The Children's Horrible House

The chil - dren's hor - i - ble house--

The chil - dren's hor - i - ble house--

Where you work all day------

And nev - er nev - er play----

The chil - dren's hor - i - ble house!

I'm sure you know this song by heart now … as all of us "Horrible" kids do.

YUP, IT'S ME AGAIN …
HOLLY … AGAIN …

FOREWORD
A FRAGMENT OF FOREVER

In the moment between seconds, when galaxies were on course for collision, a pocket within a realm came into an existence without the constraints of time, birth, or death. This pocket, made from nothing, held everything. It converged in a warp accessible only through a set time and date on earth—a cosmic interlude. The juxtaposition was ironic yet miraculously so, it could only be—just as infinity works within and outside of time and space.

The land understood while housing the divine presence along with the ancient people and animals who once roamed this sacred range. From deep inside, a signal echoed to those who could hear it, but the inhabitants who came later were deaf to its tone.

The enigmatic calescent spot was beckoning louder, now that the convergence was near, and nothing and no one could stop its purpose. The promise to escape impending doom was also a moment to return what was forbidden. But who would know or listen?

Escape from The Children's Horrible House

CHAPTER 1
Dumped

The director's lips spread into a wide menacing smile. What was that in between her teeth to the left of her incisor? Spinach? Again? I couldn't help but stare at her mouth and then her lips smacked shut.

"What are you looking at?" she snapped.

I shook my head, not wanting to antagonize her further.

"Speak!" she commanded.

"Nothing ma'am, just surprised to see you, that's all."

"Surprised, I'm sure …."

I don't know why I was surprised. *I should* expect to see Director Pankins in THE DUNGEON at The Children's Horrible House, right? I guess I was hoping to see my friends instead. After another glance, hidden in the shadows, I saw them—all of them, Clover, Staniel, and Danley, plus a small peculiar-looking girl wearing a shift that reached to the floor. They were lined up against the wall with a mix of smiles and dread on their faces. I could feel my face mirroring theirs. I looked over to Coriander, and his face said something much different. It was set in determination. Nothing would keep Coriander from accomplishing what he came here to do—that's what his face said. Good thing I'm such a good facial interpreter because his determination rubbed off on me and made me stronger, more confident in our quest. Just as I was feeling like a superhero about to beat the vile villain, lightning struck, snuffing out all of my bravery *plus* the flames. We were surrounded in spooky darkness. Suddenly, there was a massive collision of confusion. Bodies scrambled, bumped, and bounced off one another. Without warning, *my* body was lifted into the air and hoisted over someone's big strong shoulders. Children screamed, or maybe that was me, but I was pretty sure that I wasn't the only one screaming.

Where was I being taken? Who was holding me? I kicked around but then a big set of spankings on my butt kept me still.

Ouch!

I finally got them—the spankings I had been dreading, but I wasn't sure who dealt them. My butt burned as did my voice from squealing like a piglet all the way to who knows where.

Eventually I realized, it was useless to resist. The person holding me was exceptionally strong. My body bounced around atop the shoulders of the stranger while I wondered why it was still dark; then I realized I had a bag over my head and I couldn't see where I was going.

It felt like I was being transported for hours before I was finally dumped, not so gracefully, onto a cold hard surface.

"Ouch!" I said before rolling over onto the softer side of my body.

"Quiet, you wretchin' frechin' fleemin' flarmin' booger!" I heard the unmistakable growl of mean old Mr. Meanor.

I guess he didn't care for the way I had bowled him over when previously escaping from the hanging cage. I was pretty sure he would not do much to help me now. I needed to rethink my strategies so that, one: I wouldn't get caught in these situations and two, if I did find myself in these situations, I would have help getting out of them. But here I was stuck inside a big bag with no one to help me. I resigned myself to staying quiet yet hopeful. I lay still, waiting for him to cool down and, hopefully, leave.

After some time, I realized he wasn't leaving anytime soon … and there was nothing I could do. I tried to get comfortable, but my legs were starting to cramp. Things had gone from bad to really, really terrible. *What a great idea it was to come back here, Coriander.* Sarcastically, I silently blamed him for making me forget all the horrible things about this place. Why did he make me want to come back? So I could be kidnapped and tortured? What other *fun* could I possibly have? It would be *soooo* enjoyable to have those two mega jerks, Thistle and Nettle, gang up on me again, right? Maybe I could be force-fed rotten mystery meatloaf? Or clean poop-stained toilets? That sounds fun, right?

Yuck.

Something was ringing in the distance. It got louder as it got closer. After a minute or so, I heard the unmistakable sirens from a troop of firetrucks. Hopefully, they would be able to put out the fire in the glowing garden. I was suddenly filled with new hope. Maybe the firemen would break down whatever door I was behind, rescue me, take me for a ride in the truck, and we could blow the sirens all the way back to my house! *Oh*, I could play fetch with the spotted Dalmatian fire dog. I would name the dog Freckles, and he would be my new best friend. I imagined us having all kinds of fun before reality set in. What about Juniper and my friends? I couldn't leave them here. I would have to tell the fireman to get them, too; then I realized how ridiculous my thoughts were getting.

The trucks were definitely here. I heard them go past where I was being held captive then stop. What didn't stop was my urge to go tinkle. It had come on slowly, but, suddenly, I had to go badly.

"Um … Mr. Meanor, sir," I used my most polite voice. "I have to go to the bathroom," I said in a sort of muffled voice from the bag in which I was stuffed.

"Yeah, of course you do," he snickered. "You think I'm gonna fall for that wretchin' fretchin' flarmin' crap you're trying to put on me?"

"No, sir! Not that … I only have to go number one, that's all!" I tried to reassure him that I did not have to go *numero dos*—that's number two in Spanish—which translates to poopie in English.

Mr. Meanor made a questioning noise then exhaled and said, "Well, *you* … I don't believe you."

"I do! I have to go now!" I wiggled around desperately trying to hold it in. How could I prove it to him without wetting myself?

"Sure, you do."

"Mr. Meanor, if you don't take me to a toilet right now, I will go tinkle all over myself, please!" While I said this, I heard footsteps coming closer and thought it was Mr. Meanor having mercy on me.

"You gon' let her urinate herself, man?" I heard Major Whoopins' voice echoing through the chamber.

"No! I just think it's convenient timing, how she has to go now, don't you think?"

As those two were going back and forth, a couple of stray strings from the sack were sucked up into my nose and tickled the inside of my nostril. When I tried to blow them off, they tickled more and a slew of sneezes came over me.

"Havin' to go ain't never convenient, dude. Let her use the bafroom, fo' Pete's sake."

Through the torrent of sneezes, the two men argued about my use of the toilet as my need for it went away. With each sneeze, all that I was holding in, squeezed out, leaving me in a self-made puddle.

"Never mind," I said as I shamefully shook my head.

CHAPTER 2
Holly Peebody

I could tell they both knew what had happened when they became silent except for the telltale throat clearings they exchanged.

"Now go on an' look whatcha did," Major Whoopins accused.

"What *I* did?" Mr. Meanor questioned. "She's the one who just ..."

Major Whoopins cut him off and said, "Go on an' git her a new change a clothes ... *NOW*!"

I heard footsteps leave as another set came closer. The sack I was in was untied and removed. When I could see, Major Whoopins' face sheepishly smiled at mine. I felt gross and sullied. I had just soiled myself and had witnesses. I couldn't keep his gaze. My eyes fell to the ground in embarrassment.

"You gon' be alright Punkin', ya hear?" Major Whoopins assured me. I looked around the room recognizing nothing except for the exquisite workmanship that was on display in every carefully hand-crafted board and plank. Where was I? I thought I had explored every nook and cranny of The Children's Horrible House, but it seemed to be growing new rooms or buildings every time I thought

I'd seen them all. Major Whoopins used the sack to wipe up my mess while I stood helplessly. Mean old Mr. Meanor eventually came back holding a clean set of coveralls and handed them to me without even a little apology.

They both left the chamber while I changed. I really wish I could have taken a nice hot bath or shower, but that would have to wait. I was back in the white coveralls I thought I would only have to wear during my last sentence here.

My head felt weird—like it was lonely. I lifted my hands to my head to feel what was amiss when my hands landed on my hair. My hair! Where was my bunny hat??? Oh no! I looked all around but it was nowhere! It must have gotten lost in the stupid sack they had trapped me in earlier. Ugh … This same thing happened last time, too. I had to endure the arduous task of cleaning dirty rooms and making unmade beds alone, without my hat to comfort my short-haired head.

"You again," I heard echoing from the doorway behind me. I turned to see Thistle standing in the frame looking strange without her ugly, mean friend, Nettle, next to her.

I rolled my eyes feeling the last bit of nostalgia that I had once felt for this place disappear. I was at the end of my patience. I was tired, hungry, dirty, and was about to explode if one more thing set me off.

"You gon' back where you came from young lady," I heard Major Whoopins scold her as he and Mr. Hugh Mungus came back in with a mop and bucket.

"Why do you need that? What did she do, pee herthelf?" Thistle asked jokingly but when the two men looked at each other with expressions of shock, Thistle knew she had guessed correctly.

"You did! Ew …" She started to begin her assault, but Major Whoopins grabbed her by the collar and took her away as she yelled, "Bye bye, Holly Peebody!"

Mr. Mungus sloshed the mop around the room cleaning up my waste as I questioned why he would be doing something so unnecessary while a ferocious roaring fire was engulfing the estate and possibly the whole house. Why was no one panicking or trying to save the garden from being turned into a forgotten void? What about the peacocks? I hoped they were able to fly to safety.

Speaking of getting out of here, I peeked out from the door to see where I was so I could escape. I heard the unmistakable sound of children's voices echoing from what must be a large room. I realized that I was in a part of the stable house that I hadn't explored before—like I said, this horrible house seemed to continuously grow bigger and bigger.

Mr. Mungus whistled while slopping the mop to and fro. He didn't seem to be paying any attention to me so I decided this was my chance to get the heck outta here. I slid around the corner, slinking away like a cat burglar. I tiptoed at first then my feet turned into twinkle toes as I scurried over and up into the loft area. Belly down on the ground, I peered over the edge. I saw a sea of children moving like bacteria under the lens of a microscope. Thistle and Nettle caught my eye as they were jostling around some poor boy who was wearing an unnecessary pair of suspenders.

I flipped over and stared up at the vaulted wooden ceiling. The bulky rugged cross beams stretched from wall to wall like a series of bridges. Clusters of cobwebs dripped from hanging candelabras like the moss around ***The Tinsel Tree Forest*** back at my house.

BANG!!!

A loud noise sent a zapping current that shot me up like a scaredy cat. Without looking back or down, I ran for the hatch where Coriander and I had found the zip line that had taken us away from the stable house. It had dumped us out on a trail near the main house. When I opened the hatch, I reached for the handles that were not there, again. I remembered that Coriander had to find an alternative way for us to zip down, but with all these kids in here, I wouldn't be able to find anything. I stood at the edge, stuck between here and there. Here was the stable house, and there was the unknown-ish abyss.

A strong slithering scent of smoke poured into the opening. I've always loved the smell of a campfire—it reminded me of camping in the woods with my family. But this time, I knew this fire wasn't for roasting marshmallows and s'mores.

I had to get out of here. I was about to take a step toward the line to take my chances on climbing down when I felt a strong grip on my coveralls grab me back. I pulled away from whoever was trying to grab me when I lost my footing and tumbled out of the opening.

CHAPTER 3
Have A Nice Fall?

The fall felt like it lasted for an everlasting lapse in time ending with me dangling off the side of the stable house. Somehow my coveralls had snagged a hook at the ledge and held on. From my towering position, the ground was visible only when the thick fog which kept it under veil, gave way for brief pulls of air. Had I fallen, an ocean's mist or perhaps a soft cloud was waiting for me. From the way I felt in this moment, allowing myself to plummet was an acceptable solution to the hopelessness that was setting in. Would I ever break free? Fly the coop? Skedaddle?

"Grab my hand!" a voice from above spoke.

I looked up and saw only a shadow. Unsure of the trust I should employ, I looked around for any other acceptable means of escape.

"Holly! It's me! Grab my hand!" I knew the voice, now that my senses were all working together. Coriander was reaching down to me, his hand just out of reach. If I were to grab it, my coveralls might become too stretched or rip on the building which might cause me to fall. I became scared when I saw the exposed ground—

now absent of the cushioning fog. What if I fell and died? What was on the other side of life? Anything? Everything? Would I be with Falafel? Would I know if I was dead? I wasn't ready to die, I decided, as I almost lost my hold. In the nick of time, I found my hand inside Coriander's grip. He lifted me up and inside the hatch. I rolled up and over into straws of hay, breathing like I had been held under water.

"What were you doing?" Coriander asked.

"Trying to get out of here … escape," I said after a couple of thoughtful seconds.

"Looked like you were trying to get out of this whole world."

"No, just … I don't know," I exhaustedly said. I didn't have a plan and didn't know where I was headed. I just wanted to be somewhere else.

"Holly, I have bad news."

"I'm sure you do."

"The glowing garden is gone, and I think The Children's Horrible House is going to be burned to the ground."

After a little pause, all I could say was, "I hope not."

"I'm not sure if we will be able to find the treasure now," Coriander said as if this was the only thing that mattered.

I was a little baffled and perturbed by this. I didn't really care about the whole treasure like Coriander. I cared more about the fact that the most beautiful place in the universe that I had ever seen was now erased … no … burned … no … scorched from the planet.

I exhaled what little care remained. "Coriander, I couldn't care less about some stupid made-up treasure."

He looked at me like I had three heads piled high with cross-eyed snakes. He was definitely puzzled, and I didn't have enough in me to explain myself. I began to step down the ladder descending from the loft.

"Psssst," I heard Coriander call from above.

I looked up toward him, and he whispered, "You will."

CHAPTER 4
THE HUM DRUM

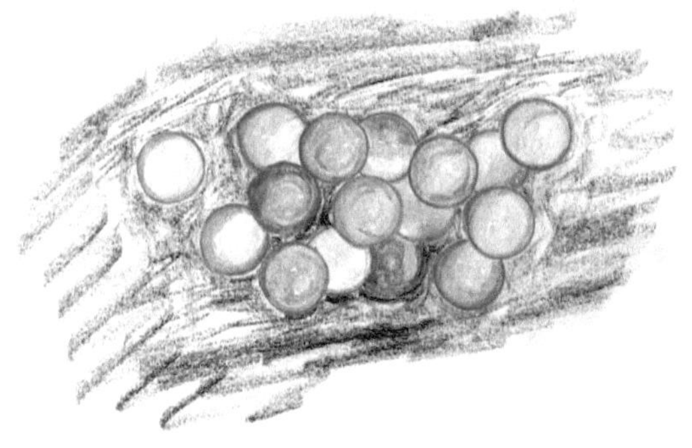

After trying to escape and find myself outside of the walls of The Children's Horrible House, I found myself right back in the routine of cleaning rooms and making beds. There was no jailbreak for me. A lot of times, it seemed no matter where I was, I wished I was somewhere else. I remember liking this place before. I remember not wanting to leave the last time I was here, except when I first arrived or when I was being punished or when I was making beds or when Thistle and Nettle bothered me or when I was stuck in THE DUNGEON. The only difference about being here this time was that I had Juniper and Begonia with me which should have made me feel better.

The Children's Horrible House was 99% saved from the massive fire that engulfed 100% of the glowing garden. But 99% of my soul went with that special place … whatever percentage that had been left over after losing Falafel. I loved that garden. There was no place on Earth as special, not even ***The Tinsel Tree Forest*** or ***The Tippy Toe Trail***.

I felt a huge loss. I silently mourned for the magical maze and the humble weeping willow tree. I wanted to howl like Falafel had for that peacock that had died under our picnic table. I couldn't even go out and look at the scorched ground that had once fertilized the magical life it had encircled.

I became reclusive only answering questions that required a "yes" or a "no" response. It was like the garden and I were both gone with Falafel. The only sound I heard clanging around in my head was the song that was sung on a daily basis:

The Children's Horrible House,
The Children's Horrible House,
Where you work all day and never, never play …
The Children's Horrible House … ahhh!

I was humming in a morbid fashion when Juniper stood in front of me while I was making my beds.

"Holly Wolly, Noddle Nolly," she said in a silly manner. I looked at her blankly then continued my chores.

"Want thome haple?" she lisped in another silly way jabbing at my poor spelling I had used in the note asking for "help" with my bed at home. That seemed like so long ago, before I knew about The Children's Horrible House.

I hummed.

"What's wrong with you?" she asked.

"Hmm, hmm, hmm, hmm, hmm, hmmmm, hmmmm, hmmmm, hmmmmmm," I hummed.

"I think you've lost your marbles, Holly," Juniper said with her eyes as big as ping pong balls.

I continued humming.

"Holly, are you okay?" she asked more seriously while gently shaking me.

I became silent for a second as I almost looked at her but then went back to humming. "Hmm, hmm, hmm, hmm, hmm, hmmmm, hmmmm, hmmmm, hmmmmmm."

"That's it, I'm taking you to see the nurse." Juniper grabbed my arm and spoke quickly to Miss Place who gave me a disgusted look, thinking I might be contagious before she waved us away.

* * *

As I was humming in the office of Miss Treetment, I overheard Juniper explaining my symptoms.

"No, she doesn't have a fever, gas, or lice. All she does is hum all day long. She even hums herself to sleep." Then I heard Juniper whisper, "I think she's lost her marbles."

"Marbles, ay? Oh, that's not good." Miss Treetment's face reflected the serious tone in Juniper's voice.

"Yeah," Juniper said.

"Let's just see here …" Miss Treetment looked around her office, lifting various files before setting them back down. Then she emptied out her trash can and sifted through the contents. She opened and closed the blinds that covered her windows. She peeked behind the medical charts then opened and closed the mouth of a hanging skeleton that served as an anatomy display. She pulled out all the tissues from her desktop box. She continued her search by opening and closing various drawers on her desk.

After some time, Juniper asked, "What are you doing?"

Miss Treetment quickly turned to look at Juniper with her impossibly thick glasses. Her huge eyes bulged when she spoke in all earnestness, "Why, I'm looking for Holly's marbles!"

I couldn't help but giggle.

Miss Treetment exclaimed, "I must have found them!" as the smile that was induced by her joke stayed visible on my face.

"Holly Hocks! You're back!" Juniper cheered.

"Hi Juniper Berries," I greeted her with sprinkles of leftover melancholy.

She hugged me tightly. "I mithed you, Holly! I thought you were going cuckoo!"

"I think I *was* going cuckoo, but thanks to you and Miss Treetment, I found my marbles."

Juniper gave me another big hug, but I still didn't feel like myself.

After a little while I said, "I'm just really sad."

"About what?" Juniper asked.

"A lot … I think … it's kind of like … a buildup … of a lot of things … and I'm just overwhelmed," I said as my eyes began to fill with tears.

"Tell me," she urged.

"Well," I sniffed, "I miss Mom and Dad, I'm still sad about Falafel, and now I've lost the glowing garden," I said. A couple of tears trickled down my cheeks as I let go of some of the burdens I'd been carrying around. The release started to help me feel better but I still had more stuff to let go. "I'm sick of jerks like Thistle and Nettle always reminding me of how ugly I am. I'm just tired of mean people and negativity. I know I'm ugly, but I can't help it. I lost my bunny hat, and I feel extra ugly without it. I wish I could just hear and see nothing sometimes. I think that's why I started humming … to block out all the stuff that was hurting me." All my woes came spilling out. After I had finished, and some time passed, I felt lighter. I felt free from the weight of my sorrows.

Juniper nodded and looked at me deeply, then she looked away. "I get it," she said and put her arm on mine. "Sometimes, it's just too much. I'm sorry, Holly. I wish I could say the right thing to make you feel better."

"You already have," I said after I blew a big grandpa-style honk into a bunch of tissues.

HONNNNK!

CHAPTER 5
Next To Nothing

Director Pankins walked through the parched path of her once thriving vivid glowing garden. The ash that settled on her shoes surrounded them as if they could breathe life back into the soil. Her heels made aerating holes with each step. What would she do now? The link between her mother and father had now been turned to dust—like their bodies, she presumed. The only thing that survived was the mausoleum where her father was supposed to be buried—*how ironic* she thought. The superior construction was impervious to the heat's destruction. It had been burned, but it stood fully intact. Even the dome-shaped planetarium was virtually unscathed. It was miraculous. The garden that had encompassed the building made it feel approachable. Now that it was in the open, not softened by mother nature, the mausoleum stood stony and desolate—not restful or habitable, especially without the peacocks still guarding it.

The birds must have escaped before or during the fire because there was no sign of them in the ashes, and they had not been seen since the day of the terrible storm that had started the fire which destroyed the garden. It was as if their watch was over.

Sirius Pankins found herself on the threshold of the tomb, unsure of her next step or direction. She looked up into the sky and saw some clouds making unusual shapes. The moment they started to look like something recognizable, they morphed into something new. But one cloud kept holding her attention longer than the rest. As it moved, she doubted her own sanity. She closed her eyes and reopened them because the picture that the cloud painted looked oddly familiar. The hair, the eyes, and mustache belonged to her father. If she had a canvas and paint, she could have recorded the image of her father exactly as the clouds had captured his likeness at this point in time.

After the image was completed, the clouds began to disintegrate. She looked down, thinking the show was over, when her gaze was called upward again. The cloud took more time to form a more intricate design. At first, Sirius couldn't tell what it was, then it began to look more familiar. The cloud became her mother, Sings-in-the-Meadow, but not just her mother, it was Saffron's image as well. She couldn't believe her eyes when it morphed to resemble young Reed Trustworthy. What was the meaning of that? Sirius closed her drying eyes. When she opened them, the clouds no longer showed a likeness to anyone or anything other than ordinary puffy clouds. She shook her head, thinking how silly she must be to visualize this nonsense when footsteps crept up from behind her. She turned to see Reed Trustworthy walking toward her.

"I thought I'd find you here."

"Were you looking for me?" she asked.

"Kind of," he coyly replied.

"What can I do for you, Reed?"

"I never thought I'd hear you ask that of me or … really anyone."

"Surprise," she said echoing his bleak tone from a while back.

Reed watched Sirius Pankins as she scanned the barren field. With each breath she exhaled, she became more and more deflated. "You know this isn't the end of the world," he offered, feeling the despair in Sirius' demeanor.

"If it gets worse from here, I'd rather that this be the end," she said.

He laughed a bit. "I can't promise that it won't be worse, but it could get better."

"Not sure how it could get better," she shrugged.

"You do know that fire is probably the best thing you can do to mature land, right?"

She obviously did not believe him.

"Fire is one of the most important elements needed for re-nourishment. The seeds and other life-giving properties re-sprout growing in abundance through the flames of fire. When this garden begins its rebirth, it will be bigger and better than ever."

Sirius pictured her garden and what it could possibly look like and feel like to be within it. Without realizing it, she found her foot drawing in the soil—mapping out a potential plan for the new garden. Reed looked down at her feet drawing lines and circles like a sidewalk artist. She bent over and used her thumb and pinky for the more delicate smudges. When she was finished some time later, she and Reed stared at the possible future. And it was out of this world.

CHAPTER 6

THE BEST DOG EVER

"Who's Falafel?" Juniper asked as we walked through the hallway toward D-Hall.

"Huh?" It felt like Falafel had been part of my family forever just like Juniper, but in actuality, he had only been with us a short period which happened to be the time that Juniper had been here looking for me. "Oh geez … where do I begin? Okay, so, Basil gave Ginger a new dog when Filbert went missing, but I decided that Falafel was *my* dog since Ginger was busy with Sugar Snap and her new litter of kittens."

"Sugar Snap had another litter of kittens? How many this time?"

"Five, I think."

"What was he like?" Juniper asked as we walked into the dining room that was warmly lit with candles and a crackling fireplace.

"Who?"

"Falafel, duh ..."

"Oh, duh ... only the best dog ever, if you can imagine." I was sure no descriptions could capture him completely, but I gave it a shot as we stood in line to get our trays of food. "He was the cutest little puppy!" My voice got higher as I described him. "His fur was light sand, and his eyes were blue and brown." Juniper scrunched her nose so I elaborated. "He had one ice-blue eye and one root-beer-brown eye but both were tender like his heart. He never pooped in the yard, and he followed me around wherever I went."

"What happened to him?" Juniper asked as we walked toward Staniel and Danley's table that was much bigger than the usual four-top we used to share. Our group was expanding.

"Someone shot him," I said as I plopped my tray down.

"Whoa! What are you guys talking about?" Danley asked.

"Sounds pretty serious," Staniel said.

"My dog, Falafel."

"Oh, someone shot him? Who?" Danley asked.

"Wish I knew."

"You don't know who did it?" Juniper asked.

"I think it was Mr. Painintheas."

Juniper gasped and covered her mouth. The table became silent until Clover walked over with the little girl I had seen her with when Director Pankins captured me in THE DUNGEON. Since I had lost my marbles or become more or less absent from my body, I hadn't been sensible enough to ask about her. She had a sweet face with a kind demeanor, but there was something peculiar about the way she carried herself. She almost looked unreal or magical—like a pixie. I saw the twins trying not to stare at her, but they just couldn't help it. Right away the girl started to eat, and as the bulge in her cheeks moved up and down, her uniquely-shaped, blue-colored eyes turned to me.

"Hi Juniper's sister, I'm Déjeuner, Juniper's bestest friend. I hear Clover is yours!" Begonia was walking over to our table and cleared her throat indicating that she, Begonia, my *new* best friend, had arrived.

"Eh hem, why yes, yes. *I* am Holly's best friend. Pleasure to meet you," Begonia said seriously but masqueraded her statement as sarcasm. Clover's eyebrows rose and then softened again when I gave her a reassuring smile. Déjeuner tilted her head and continued to chew until she gulped down her food and followed it with a big swig of milk. She wiped off her dripping mustache and smiled, exposing a mouthful of big white teeth.

"Hi Déjeuner, nice to meet you; my name's Holly."

"Holly Peebody, Holly Peebody, couldn't hold it in so she peed all over her body," Thistle and Nettle sang as they came close to our table before going to sit at their own empty table. No one was waiting for them, not even Cherry, whom I hadn't seen at all since my arrival. Thistle and Nettle were thrilled with their lame song and gave each other a high-five before they filled the air with their gloating guffaws.

My face fell. I wasn't ready for their assaults so soon. I was just barely feeling better from the brink of despair. How much more could I take? Juniper calmly stood and walked over to their table. I could see her talking to them with an expression that I had never seen her display. She got in their faces while looking nice but serious. She stuck her index finger in each one of their chests and in their faces, then gave them an opportunity to respond. After a second they both nodded, and she said, "Good."

As she walked back over to me, she smiled triumphantly. "You won't be bothered by those two anymore."

"What did you say?" I asked.

"You don't need to know exactly, but let's just suppose I told them that if they messed with you again, they would find themselves sleeping inside Hawthorne North Star's tomb with his worm infested skeleton."

We shared a devilish grin and giggle while imagining those two butt-brains buried within the grave. They wouldn't be so brave then. Clover, the twins, and I had already seen inside Hawthorne's tomb, and it wasn't what we had expected, at all. The four of us looked at each other and mentally found ourselves back inside Hawthorne North Star's mausoleum—our smiles faded. Coriander had been there with us, too, but he wasn't sitting with us today at lunch. Where was he? He did this before. I knew what he was doing but never sure of how or where he was operating. He was on a secret mission while he was here which at times included me. When it didn't include me, I wondered what he was finding.

CHAPTER 7
The Hardest Part

Miss Judge, who was always searching and researching, worked best alone. At times she worked alongside the director, Sirius Pankins, to allow her to feel included.

With the two books, *Sage Themes* and *The Message,* now together, at last, Miss Judge examined every detail within the texts and felt close to attaining her goal. Inside the security of her thoughts, she was pensively gloating over the connections that she had put together, and she almost felt guilty for not sharing her information with anyone—but if they wouldn't work hard enough to figure this out, then they didn't deserve to share in the spoils.

She dreamed of the day the treasure would be found and the triumphant feeling she would possess. She would no longer be confined to her attic-like dwelling, and she would have the entire estate to herself. But would she still want this life of solitary confinement? On some level, she felt a connection to this strange group of people. She knew that she wanted more than they could offer, but what would fulfill her? What would she do if she had no limits?

During her reverie, her cat, Copernicus, slithered between her legs and gave her a vibrating meow indicating that he would like some attention. She reached down, picked him up, and pet his head while he gratefully purred. While she caressed him, her mind returned to its quest. She realized that at this point maybe all she had to do was wait, but that was the hardest part … waiting, all alone. Perhaps she should find an ally.

CHAPTER 8
A WHAT?

Dramatic organ music blared throughout the halls as all the kids were corralled into the large formal ballroom melded together by the grated windows that stretched floor to ceiling. Rectangular sunbeams shone through the glass stretching across the elegant room. Within the shadows upon the stage stood many of the horrible house staff. There was something strange about Director Pankins. Begonia and I stood together while all the children were gathered in an assembly similar to when I had first arrived. Instead of being stern or intimidating, the director seemed solemn and thoughtful. None of us had ever witnessed Director Pankins in such a state. Her eyes were cast down but when the music stopped, with an overly dramatic bang, she looked up at all of us staring at her.

She cleared her throat. "Many years ago I drew up plans for a garden," her voice wavered as if an emotion came over her. "To my surprise, those plans came to fruition. It was a place no one deserved to enjoy because it was too wonderful. You may recall my beloved glowing garden. That place has been destroyed and …" she paused as the room stayed silent. The children, staff, and I hung on her every word. "Well, there is only one thing we can do about it."

What was it? What could we do about it?

"Look here, children," she said as a giant piece of material unfolded until large scrolled-letters spelled, "ENCHANTMENT OF THE STARS". She explained her proposal to revitalize the grounds at The Children's Horrible House and how we were going to employ every bit of all the subject matter we had studied here to fulfill the plans. Miss Spelling, Miss Guide, and Miss Leads were all up on the stage while she spoke.

Everyone *oohed* and *ahhed* based on the clever space-themed artwork of the banner. After comparing the activities that were similar to the previous year's celebration, it did look interesting.

It was an event that would occur on the next Star Day Celebration. I had remembered Miss Spelling telling us that this year's stellar conjunction would be even more spectacular than the one we had witnessed previously. The last one was so cool; I couldn't imagine it could be any better. But since I was only able to attend the last part of the Star Day Celebration—the stellar conjunction, perhaps, I might actually be able to participate in all the activities this year. I started to get excited … until … .

There was a catch. There was always a catch. In order for us to deserve this evening of enchantment, we would have to work for it. On the other side of the director's podium, another banner unfolded. On it was a plan for a new garden, called The Children's Horrible Garden. It sounded, how can I put this … *Horrible???* But in truth, it didn't look so bad. This garden was intended to be bigger and possibly better than the last. At least that's how it looked.

"As you all know, the fire destroyed a beautiful and sentimental place. But, children … all is not lost. There is hope. We can and we will rebuild what we have lost. And it will be a place big enough for all of us to get lost inside. It will be called The Children's Horrible Garden where we will work all day and even have time to play … if you do your work!"

I have to admit, it sounded promising. "Time to play …" echoed in my brain.

"Take a look at these spots." She pointed to several empty areas on the plan. "These are where each group will work, and, because I am so generous, I will allow each of you to plan your own unique theme within this horrible garden. It will be your very own." I looked around to see the kids' expressions. I had never seen confusion in such massive quantity. It seemed that every child had become enthralled yet befuddled by the thought of having some kind of ownership in this *horrible* garden. I, myself, never thought about having any kind of say here at The Children's Horrible House … and I'm pretty sure none of these other kids did either.

"You can do whatever you want with your horrible space." The director had a knack for reading my thoughts during these assemblies. "You can put in a dead fish pond and gargoyle sculptures or a game of some sort or just make a place to think horrible thoughts and rest. But we will all be working together in teams. Who's with me?"

All the children cheered even though I'm sure they were not sure why they were cheering. I cheered, too. But something bothered me—the way she spoke, her facial expressions, enthusiasm about a horrible garden??? Who was this woman, and where was the old spinach-toothed dragon-lady, Director Sirius Pankins? No one else seemed suspicious except for one face. With his arms crossed underneath a skeptical expression, Coriander stood doubtfully across the room.

He looked at me briefly before I started to wave. He turned away, becoming lost in the crowd. My hand stuck in waving position was let back down but not before a goofy boy picking his nose made eye contact and thought I was waving at him. He pulled his finger out from his nostril and showed me his prize. I hoped no one caught me waving to the booger boy and his booger. How embarrassing!

Where did Coriander go? Was he mad at me? I wondered what I could have done and almost got mad at him for possibly being mad at me for no good reason when I felt a tap on my right shoulder. I turned to see emptiness behind me so I turned back around. Another tap on my left shoulder caused me to turn to the left behind me but no one was there again. Then a tap on each of my shoulders and a guilty giggle caused me to turn to see Coriander covering his mouth that was smiling at his trickery.

I forgot about the old tap-on-the-shoulder-trick game, then I remembered one of my own. I pointed to an imaginary stain on his shirt and asked, "What's that?" When he looked down to investigate, I used my index finger to slide up and "boop" his nose. He, then I giggled and casually hid our sly fox smiles.

"Where have you been?" I whispered.

"You know … here and there … everywhere."

"Ha ha. Seriously, I haven't seen you in forever."

"It's been a little while but not *that* long."

"You're always so vague," I taunted.

"You're always exaggerating." He got me on that one.

"Touché."

"Some speech, huh?" I asked, hoping to stoke an actual conversation.

"I guess so," he said consistently.

"What do you think of all this? A Children's Horrible Garden?" I prodded.

"I think it's a *horrible* idea," he said in a mocking tone, then added, "Honestly, I have no idea, but I will never trust her. There's something not right about all this. I think she's up to something. Maybe she is still searching for the treasure and needs our help by pretending to allow us to work for her. I don't see why all these other kids can't see her for who she really is."

"Who is she, really?" I asked hoping that he would tell me something I hadn't thought of.

"Who really knows? But, I do know *this is* not her."

Again … he was vague. What wasn't vague was something the

director said during her speech that surprised me. It was something I never knew about her, and I went on to think about it the rest of the day.

CHAPTER 9
A Drift To Slumberland

Juniper insisted on giving me back my bunk while she slept in the bunk beds closest to mine, directly above Déjeuner. Begonia was in Clover's room which made things feel weird between us. I saw her less and less with all the new friends she was making.

I could hear my sister and Déjeuner talking softly as I stared out of the window. The stars twinkled as the sickle moon smiled like the Cheshire Cat from *Alice in Wonderland*. I imagined the entire striped cat with his curved tail emerging around the grin of the moon. A red light off in the distance blinked before it vanished. Had I imagined it? I searched for it again, but it never flashed.

After my sister and Déjeuner fell asleep, the house became absurdly quiet. Without the cries from the peacocks, the only sound I could hear was the heavy inhalation and exhalation that the house made, especially at night. This horrible house was alive but its breathing was labored as if it was sad. Maybe it was exhausted after almost being burned to the ground, or maybe it missed its garden. I missed it, too, and suddenly felt bad for the house losing its closest companion.

What would I do if I lost my closest companion? Oh yeah … I did. I had just lost my dog, Falafel. I had never felt more alone. This house and I had gone through a terrible tragedy. I became in tune with the home's expressive breathing. I knew this off-beat rhythm all too well. When I felt extra lonesome, weeks after Falafel died, I sniffled, hiccupped, and fought to breathe while I cried for him. It seemed the house was doing the same. Maybe I could comfort it the way my mom had comforted me. She would sit with me allowing me to cry without saying much. Just her being next to me had made me feel better. *What could I do to help The Children's Horrible House?* I was here, but did it know? Then I remembered Director Pankins' idea about the new bigger, better horrible garden. No dog could ever replace Falafel just as no garden could be as magical as the glowing garden. Perhaps a newer, bigger, better one might ease the pain that the house was experiencing. How could I make this garden not so horrible and possibly better than the last one? Could it even be possible? That place was an original piece of perfection! What could *I* do that would be as magical? My brain started to hurt as it labored to think. Maybe my brain was tired too. I decided to not think and just sort of go to a place in my head where thoughts could lie still—be suspended. It's next to impossible because thoughts always drift … and … drift … and … drift … until … sleep.

Next thing I knew, I was surrounded by trickles of light feathering around my face in dappled dots. Drops of dew cascaded down my cheeks. Everything around me grew into a living space that felt abundant, yet surreal. I was surrounded by giant blades of grass and brilliant bulging blooms bigger than the sun. Polka dotted red mushrooms grew higher and wider than the trees I loved to climb. It seemed that I was the size of an ant, or I was in a garden that belonged to a giant. A loud buzz went past. Two sparkling green dragonflies the size of fighter jets flickered through the ground cover. They made a loud clicking noise as a large lady bug bounced into the foray causing a big black beetle to flip over onto his back. His wiry legs squirmed as he lay on the ground. I ran over to him. His grabby front mouth pincers scared me at first so I jumped back. I went to his side after realizing his mobility was severely limited. I pushed on his bulbous body hoping to flip him over, but I wasn't strong enough. I pushed as hard as I could but barely lifted him at all. I heard a tiny voice coming from him asking me to push again so I did, and this time he flipped over quite easily.

I became very proud of myself until I saw that it wasn't my brute strength that had aided the beetle, but a strong caterpillar who happened to scoot by at the right time. The caterpillar was traveling like a train through a tunnel. I watched him as my eyes tried to keep up with each spiracle as it passed. *Choo Choo*! A whistle floated up and echoed around. I never knew caterpillars could whistle. It chug-a-chug-chugged, whistled again and again until I woke up.

The whistle did not come from the caterpillar; it was the train that passed by in the distance from The Children's Horrible House. The house gently shook in response to the train's call. It sounded unusually loud as it rumbled past. Maybe the wind was carrying its revolving thud prints farther than usual.

Nighttime was still draped across the sky, and I was extra tired, but when I fell back to sleep, my slumber seemed to last for only a minute before I was startled by those dreadful morning bells.

CHAPTER 10
Miss Spelling's Metamorphosis

After morning work, which seemed to fly by because I had become such an ace at making these blasted beds and cleaning these stinkin' rooms, we went to class. Miss Spelling was still my favorite teacher of all time, and she didn't disappoint today. We learned about how the fire that seemed so destructive to our glowing garden might have been the best thing for it. It would be a new beginning.

She went through a couple of different life forms that have new beginnings like frogs from tadpoles and butterflies from caterpillars. She called this metamorphosis.

"Does anyone know what that word means or has anyone ever heard the term before?" Miss Spelling asked.

"My aunt read me a story called *The Metamorphosis* when I was staying at her house. It was all about this dude that woke up as a cockroach and his parents were all like *EWWWWWW,* and then everybody was all like e*wwwwww*," a boy nicknamed Bloomer said while acting out the scene with exaggerated hand gestures.

"Well, that's not exactly what I'm talking about. *But* on second thought, maybe the story of Gregor Samsa from *The Metamorphosis* could be closer than I first thought!" Miss Spelling exclaimed, seemingly as surprised as the boy who offered what he supposed was the wrong answer.

"Yeah, Gregor, that was the dude's name!" Bloomer called out.

Miss Spelling nodded and continued with her lesson. "Metamorphosis comes from the Greek word *meta* meaning *change* and *morphe* meaning *form*, hence change form."

"That's what the dude did! He turned from a human to a roach!" he blurted.

"Yes, yes, but did you know that animals and plants do that too? Some start out with one form then they change to another as part of their overall design." Miss Spelling paused briefly to let what she had said sink in.

"Take for instance the metamorphosis in amphibians which is made possible through a hormone called thyroxin. This process is dependent upon the concentrations of this hormone inside a tadpole which, by the way, originated as an egg, then transformed into larvae, then, through using said hormone, brings about a metamorphosis. Then there is prolactin which is a protein that counteracts the hormone's effect. The outcome of the metamorphosis is influenced by many different variables such as the environment in which it grows or the ecological conditions surrounding it. Because of this, tadpoles can develop in different ways—they are all unique with distinct variations—*if* you look closely … just like each of you," she said with a wink.

"Certain tadpoles can have horny ridges for teeth, whiskers, and fins. They also have a lateral organ line for their senses, but after metamorphosis, these organs are no longer necessary and will be reabsorbed by controlled cell death."

The class was quiet as all her words echoed in our minds. The information bounced around before implanting a sense of what Miss Spelling was trying to teach us.

"Does this same thing happen to roaches?" Bloomer asked.

"Well, sort of... cockroaches undergo egg and nymphal stages before becoming adults, but it's not the same thing. Humans, too, start out as an egg, so to speak. But, on to another subject, let's talk about matter."

Miss Spelling walked to her desk and picked up a hunk of clay. "Does anyone know what matter is?" she asked.

"Is it clay?" a girl named Zephyr asked.

"Yes ... and ...?"

No one knew what she wanted so we waited.

"What's the matter with you?" Miss Spelling chuckled after her attempt at a joke. As a courtesy, we gave her some gratification with a "ha ha".

"Everything that's anything is matter! You're matter, I'm matter, this desk is matter, this house is matter, the foundation this house sits upon is matter!" she said with excitement. "And matter cannot be created nor destroyed. It can only be turned into something new."

"So matter can metamorphosis?" I asked bumbling the pronunciation.

"That's the incorrect term but, yes! The correct way to say it is metamorphosize. Remember how the garden was destroyed by the fire?"

"Yes," a few of us answered collectively.

"Well, it didn't just disappear. It turned into something new because it was made of matter. With our help, it can be designed into something even better than before."

"Maybe we'll make it look like a giant cockroach, and we'll call it the Gregor Garden," Bloomer said proudly.

"Don't think so," Miss Spelling shook her head. "Does anyone have any other ideas?"

The children started calling out their genius ideas.

"We could turn it into a clubhouse for boys, and no girls would be allowed."

"No, we could turn it into a tea house where we would have tea time and bake biscuits!"

"I'll eat the biscuits," Bloomer said before he looped his tongue around his lips.

"How about a baseball field!"

"No, a bowling alley!"

"That's not exactly what I meant, but hey, maybe we could make variations on those ideas." The class breathed a collective groan. "Under Director Pankins' authority, we have been given an opportunity to each have a say in how we can plan, design, and cultivate our very own Children's Growing Garden."

Growing garden … I repeated to myself. It sounded much better than the Children's Horrible Garden and almost just like the glowing garden—instead of the letter *l*, there was an *r* after the *G*, making a profound difference … from just one letter.

CHAPTER 11
Formality Versus Family

The library doors swung open, and the director marched over to the wall of books, found a flimsy paperback that appeared to be of little consequence and tugged on it. After the camouflaged door opened, she waltzed into the hidden chamber then stood at the base of the spiral stairs and beckoned for the librarian. While she waited, Copernicus, Willow's cat, peered over the edge and rubbed his neck on the railing as well as every other object that requested his scent.

The cat prowled down the steps coming face to face with Miss Pankins. He stuck his head out for her to pet. When she tried to abstain, he meowed imploringly—a sound she couldn't resist. Her hand lifted to his soft, fuzzy head. He moved around so she could pet him more. Soft purring echoed from his motor that had a relaxing effect on her. But she was not here to relax. She was here to take care of some serious business. She stopped petting Copper and redirected her mission.

"Miss Judge!"

"Why do you insist on calling for me so formally? Willow is my name; you know that; I know that; everyone knows that."

Ignoring the librarian's request, Director Pankins went straight to the point.

Willow walked past the director and into the library while the director laid out her plans.

"It's time we start getting more serious. I feel like we are under some sort of time constraint. My gut is telling me that it has something to do with this next Star Day. If we don't have our mission formulated by then, I'm afraid it may be our last chance to figure this out."

For once the sisters agreed. With all the secret research and putting their heads together, things were culminating. These events could lead to answers but the right questions had to be asked. Whatever was waiting for them—treasure, inheritance, or closure wouldn't be easy to obtain.

"I wish I could trust Reed. I feel like he's not who he says he is," Willow said.

Miss Pankins twitched her eyebrows down in thought briefly. "Well, I don't know about him. What I do know is that we need to keep our focus locked on those kids, particularly Holly Spinatsch. The moment I laid my eyes on her, she looked back at me with no ordinary expression. I knew there was something strange, and it wasn't just her ungainly appearance or her unusual bunny hat."

The director put her hand up to her determined chin, pensively moving her thumb and index finger around it. "Actually, she seemed inconsequential until after I sent her home. That's when I realized that she would be useful to our mission; I just wasn't sure how."

"In what way are you supposing?" Willow asked while restocking some books, trying to not notice the directors slight change in demeanor.

Miss Pankins noticed how Willow took her time finding the exact places where each book belonged—it annoyed the director. She wanted progress, results, not books placed in the correct order.

"Give those to me," Miss Pankins grabbed the books, putting them aside so she could have Willow's full attention. "I just said I don't know, but you aren't paying attention!"

Willow looked at Sirius, thinking of many different things to say but, instead, patiently asked, "Are you planning to examine her?" This seemed to distract the director. She looked away, likely picturing the occasion. In her thoughtful moments, Willow found the director's sharp profile quite stunning, but when Sirius fixed her radiating amber eyes on her or anyone, she looked like a hunting lone wolf that could not be trusted.

"Soon. *She* knows something, plus *we* have figured out a whole lot of … of … squat," the director growled.

Willow, ever optimistic, thought briefly before saying, "I wouldn't exactly say … squat."

"Okay, then tell me, do you know how to find where our beloved parents left our inheritance?" Miss Pankins asked while her hands jolted upwards.

"Well, not exactly, but I think we are closer to figuring it out now than we were before."

"Before when?" Miss Pankins began to pace back and forth.

"Let's see …" Willow picked up one of the books that Miss Pankins had cast aside and thought about where it belonged while the director continued her brainstorming. "Before Holly Spinatsch and her gang exposed our father's empty grave?"

"Yes, since then. What have we put together after that?"

Willow was silent as she flipped through the pages of the innocuous book.

"Squat," the director answered for her.

Silence again.

"Exactly," Miss Pankins said as she grabbed the book out of Willow's hand and threw it across the room.

CHAPTER 12
GETTIN' SENTIMENTAL

After class that day, I thought about how the new garden might look. It would take forever for it to mature into something like the glowing garden. I would probably never get to see the new horrible growing garden in its fullness, ever. I felt hopeless and discouraged. I still longed for the glowing garden. I couldn't let it go. I wanted to bring some part, if not all of it, back like it was before. I overheard the other kids talking about boring stuff. None of them seemed to care about what used to be there. All they cared about was … *oh, who knows what*?

I felt a tap on my shoulder. I turned, thinking that someone was trying to play a trick on me. But I was wrong. Clover stood smiling at me in an extra warm way.

"Hi strangah," she greeted.

"Clover! How are you?" I didn't hesitate to give her a big hug. Even though I had been here for a little while, Clover and I never seemed to have any time where it was just the two of us.

"Now, don't get all sentimental on me," she teased.

"I can't help it. Guess I missed you … a lot."

"Can't say I blame ya," she said with a sly side smirk. "I am pretty great!"

"I got really worried there for a while when I was back home."

"Worried, at home? Why?"

"'Cause I lost my dog, and I thought you might not want to come over if I didn't have my dog, Filbert. And … and our dogs couldn't have that puppy playdate that we had planned. Oh … I got a new dog named Falafel but then he died. I was so sad, I cried for days." My face fell along with my pride.

After I said all that, I realized how pathetic I sounded. It would be great if I could put all those words back in my mouth, swallow them, then dispose of them into the pathetic-sounding sentence dumpster.

Clover tilted her head, "You think that's the only reason why we're friends? Our dogs that have nevah met?" she asked.

I felt even more stupid. "No … I mean … well, that did occur to me."

"Holly, I'm not your friend because of anything like that, I'm your friend because it's easy."

"Huh?"

"Good friends are good friends because when you're with 'em, it's easy. It's not work or somethin' we need to have an excuse for. Even though I haven't seen you in a while, I still know we're friends. We're friends because we just are. Does that make sense?"

I wondered why some people were more comfortable around certain people. Was it energy or magnetism or gravitational pull like our planets that hung together in the solar system? Were the planets all best friends like me, Coriander, Clover, the twins, Conifer, Juniper, Begonia, and Déjeuner? Nine friends and nine planets, could that be a coinkydink?

"Perfect sense," I said. "By the way, I found my dog Filbert, after all, so we can still have our puppy playdate."

She giggled and rolled her eyes. "That would be great. Now if we can just get outta this horrible house."

"I'm a little homesick," I confessed.

"*You* think you're homesick! I almost can't remembah my family, it's been so long since I've seen 'em."

I knew very little about Clover's family except for the little things she told me here and there about her dog and how she was the only blonde-haired, blue-eyed one in her family. Her parents and siblings all had dark brown hair and eyes.

"Do you think they would recognize you, being so grown up and all?" I asked teasing her about her longer hair that had grown out from the mullet-style it had been when I first met her.

Clover looked around then down. When she peeked up at me, I wasn't sure but it looked like her eyes began to gloss over, "Actually, I'm not even sure if they care." She blinked heavily to keep her tears from escaping.

"What do you mean?"

"I kinda like bein' here more than home, to be honest with you, Holly."

What? Who would prefer this spooky, overloaded with work, disgusting food, poop-smelling heap over home? "Why is that?" I asked, clearly puzzled.

"Well, before I left home, my parents were in the middle of gettin' a divorce, and they were bein' really mean to each otha. They kinda stopped carin' about bein' parents; which is why our house, especially my room, became extra messy. I didn't see any reason to make my bed. I was kinda askin' to be taken to The Children's Horrible House. I felt stuck in the middle between my mom and dad, like I had to pick sides. I didn't want to have to hurt eitha one of my parents so when I came here, I didn't have to choose."

"You weren't scared to come here?" *Like I was?* Is what I was thinking.

"A little, but after what I've been through, I didn't care."

"Do you get along with your parents?"

"Yes, I love my mom and dad very much, but they don't like each otha. They want us to choose between 'em, and I just can't. It's like choosin' which arm you like bettah. I need both of my arms."

Yikes, I thought. I looked down at both of my arms realizing I never appreciated them as much as I did right then. I would hate to lose any part of my body. I understood how Clover was feeling—parents are a part of us. They're why we are the way we are. I felt bad for Clover; she didn't even have a whole family waiting for her back home. I thought about my family, how weird everyone was in their own ways but thinking that divorce could change that made me become grateful for everything—my dad's old jalopies that made him so happy, my mom's singsong voice being grateful after she farted, Hickory's constant noises from both ends, Cashew's sweet reassurances about how I wouldn't be ugly forever, Juniper's crazy accents, even Ginger's sophisticated insults. At least we were all together—a family.

"Clover, if we ever get to leave, you could stay with me and my family, if you want," I said as I used both of my arms to hug her.

She let out a big breath of air, releasing her tension. I could tell she was trying to decide what to say when Begonia slid up with Dookie poking out of her coverall pocket.

"Dookie! Come here you little scoop of butterscotch pudding puff!" I grabbed him out of her pocket, nuzzled him while Clover and Begonia talked about a situation that happened in their room with a girl that I didn't know very well, *and* Thistle and Nettle, *of course*. I had zero interest in any conversation about those two sphincters (I used one of my sister's clever words to silently insult them). Instead, I snuggled with Dookie until they said something that I couldn't pretend to ignore.

"I think they're nice. Well, at least they're nice to me," Begonia shrugged.

"Who?" I asked hoping that what I heard was wrong.

"Thistle and Nettle. They've been showing me around and giving me tips on how to stay out of trouble," Begonia said with utter sincerity. What wasn't sincere, were those two creepy clown-faced gargoyles. What were they up to? Were they trying to steal Begonia away from me as they had almost accomplished with Clover? Were they trying to get to me through my friends? What was their motive for being so nice to *my* friends?

"Those two are not the kind of girls you should get advice from. They are just using you," I said.

"For what?"

"To get to me," I said.

Begonia's sassy side came out, "Again, I'll ask … for what?"

I couldn't say for sure how they were using her to get to me but I knew there was something. I could feel it, but instead I said, "I don't know."

"Okay, well I think they're nice, and until I see otherwise, I'll give them a chance."

I don't think you should, is what I was thinking but I knew Begonia too well. If I tried to tell her what to do, that ornery side of her would rebel so I stayed silent … even though I wanted to ***SCREAM!***

CHAPTER 13
STAR FALL

Later that night in the dining hall, I was sitting with all my friends. It felt good to be with everyone. Begonia and Clover were smiling while they took turns feeding Dookie who was getting so big! The twins were stealing food from preoccupied diners like Clover and Begonia. Juniper and Déjeuner were playing a hand slap game that Déjeuner seemed to win even though Juniper had an obvious sight advantage that was letting her down so treacherously. Coriander was absent as usual, but I knew he was safe and definitely up to something.

The fire in the hearth was strong, and the chill in the air kept a perfect balance of comfort. The warm-colored walls accented by the unending display of paintings made the dwelling much less spooky than the outside of the house. From within the walls, the people in the paintings made the house feel inhabited not just by us kids and the staff—as if a legacy lived here and was carried on by these portraits.

I felt rich, borderline spoiled yet consoled by the fact that I earned my keep around this luxurious peculiar home. As I went to bed, my capricious thoughts continued. I lay within the covers staring at nothing in particular. This horrible house oftentimes felt so homey that when something truly out of the ordinary occurred, I almost didn't notice until it became impossible to not see it.

Sorry about all my rambling … You're probably wondering what I'm talking about, aren't you? Well, I was so uncertain about the reality of what was happening that I almost couldn't believe it myself.

Okay, I'll tell you.

So, I was sitting in my bed, the last bed in the chamber right next to the window, when the stars began to fall from the sky. They didn't just stream through the night sky and disappear into the darkness; they fell toward the Earth hitting the ground like super-solid glowing snowballs, but these were not made of snow even though they melted into the ground shortly after their plummet. I got up and ran through the squeaking, creaking, exhaling house, not thinking about how I would get outside or the consequences of being caught. As if I had been magically teleported, I was alone outside with my gaze drawn upward.

The sky glowed with what looked like the lanterns that we had sent up into the sky on Star Day coming down in bulbs of light with trails of glitter gently hitting the ground, planting themselves within the soil where the glowing garden once was. The ground became illuminated in dots. As I walked around, the light grew around my feet. With each step I took, the field lit up as if the soil itself were alive, filled with stars, swimming through the ground while more and more stars dribbled from the heavens. I looked up, closed my eyes, holding out my hands hoping to catch one while my body began to sway with the mystical tune that the falling stars made with each drop.

The warm amber light was beaming into my eyelids. My whole being began to feel as if it was entering another dimension, where the realities I once relied upon no longer held constraints—where thoughts were suspended or where anything was possible. I must be dreaming, I told myself. When I opened my eyes, I was stunned to find that I was not in my bed or dreaming nor was I in my room nor was I normal. Yes, I know I've never been *normal*, but this was quite exceptional.

When I looked at my hands, my feet, and then the rest of my body, I was glowing like the stars that were falling from the sky—they were swimming around under my skin! I felt an exciting feeling like I had just become one with the universe—like I was a supernatural being. I waved my hands around noticing a trail of light following my movements fading into glitter. Maybe I was a human comet. I ran around to see if I left a trail of light. What an amazing feeling! I couldn't wait to show everyone my new spectacular superpower. I turned to look at The Children's Horrible House to see that it too was glowing. I wondered if everyone else now had the same powers that I had been given.

But just when I was feeling extra awesome, the falling stars turned into a mist that felt like rain. In fact, it *was* rain and it continued for some time. Sadly, the dampness snuffed out the glowing stars that sunk deeper into the soil. The house and soil became dark and gloomy again. When I regarded myself, I saw that my inner light was now diminished as well.

Phooey.

I slumped my shoulders, walked my ordinary self back to the ordinary spooky house, up to my dull room, soaking wet, and resigned myself to bleakness. After I dried myself, I climbed into bed and drifted off to sleep … until …

CHAPTER 14
Missed Blessings

From her overlook, Sirius Pankins watched as her pupil was showered and empowered by what could only be explained as a cosmic intervention. The fantastic display was something that no one's wildest imagination could fathom. It appeared that the universe sprinkled its magical stardust over the girl and into the earth. Why didn't she wake up sooner so it could have happened to her?

She had been awakened by the streams of light, but when she looked out her window, Holly was already outside being sprinkled in the star shower. Sirius felt a weird jealousy over something that Holly simply had inside her. Holly probably couldn't help it, she thought. What was it about Holly that had Sirius so curious and perplexed? Could she be jealous over someone who was obviously inferior and appeared to be of little substance? What did Holly Spinatsch have that she did not?

Sirius watched as the afterglow that was once so luminous began to fade. As Holly stood and looked around, she appeared to be normal as ever—out-of-place, unkempt, gawky, and a tad too tall—same as always. Maybe Holly Spinatsch wasn't so special, after all … so she told herself. But it wouldn't hurt to find out for certain.

CHAPTER 15
Have A Look

I was shaken … then shaken harder … my eyes fluttered and closed. The shaking started again, but this time when I opened my eyes, I stared into the round cavities of Miss Place's nostrils which flared open while she shook me more. There was nothing more unsettling than something so hideous waking you.

"I'm awake," I stated as I turned away from her yucky, hairy, booger barrels.

"Let's go!" Miss Place gave me only a second to grab some things before she escorted me to the director's office. I hadn't gone to the bathroom or eaten breakfast, and my eyes were crusty. So, when Director Pankins' face and mouth snarled at my appearance, I was not surprised. However, I was startled to see Miss Judge, the librarian, in the director's office.

"Hello Holly," Miss Judge smiled. Her deep-set warm brown eyes crinkled at the edges as she held her expression. She was pretty, especially when she smiled. The lipstick she wore matched her flaming lava hair while her straight teeth filled her smiling mouth like small pillars of chalk.

Somehow I was a sucker for her reassuring simper, though I was not sure I could trust her. The last time I had seen her, she had unveiled her true identity to be Willow Faint Star, Director Pankins' half-sister. And Director Pankins was actually Saffron Radiant Star, both daughters and heirs of Hawthorne North Star, the founder of The Hawthorne House for Children which later became known as The Children's Horrible House.

What's with this family and their secret identities? I understand a nickname but c'mon, this was getting ridiculous. On second thought, I remember my mom explaining nicknames to me when I was a lot younger—like a couple of years or so ago … *maybe more*, I don't know.

My mother explained that my grandfather's real name was Walter but his nickname was Walt and that my grandmother's real name was Frances but her nickname was Franny. After some thought, I asked, since my name was Holly, could my nickname be Petunia? She laughed and said, "That's not exactly how it works, honey, but sure, your nickname can be Petunia." For some reason, no one ever called me Petunia. Guess I looked more like a Holly Hocks.

"Hi, Miss Judge," I sleepily said as I scooped away some eye boogers.

"Have a seat, will you?" She indicated an empty chair in front of the two books that had caused so much mischief the last time I had been here, *The Message* and *Sage Themes*. I sat down, immediately feeling small in the prodigious chair.

"Remember these?" she asked in an unusual tone.

I looked at the books, back at her, and then at Director Pankins who grimaced in an unnatural fashion.

I nodded.

"Have a look, won't you?"

I was confused. What did they want from me?

"Go on! Open them!" the director prodded.

I put my hand over the cover of *Sage Themes,* briefly noting the thick embossed leather and gold lettering. In the corners were different plants, and in the upper middle part, the solar cross was clearly outlined. I opened the heavy book, flipped through the animal skin pages, but still saw only what I had seen before—a lot of words, dates and drawings.

After some browsing, pretending to examine both books, I shrugged and looked up at them for their next command.

"What do you see?" Miss Judge asked.

What was I supposed to see? I wondered as I scratched my head.

"Ummm, just like … well, it all just looks like words, dates, and pictures."

"Look harder," the director ordered.

I looked harder and pulled my glasses up closer to my face so I could see better. After a while I could tell that the ladies were becoming impatient. My eyes began to hurt. As I took off my glasses to clean them as well as give my eyes a break, not only did the 3D images pop out from the book, they also appeared to be in motion. If I wasn't mistaken, they were holograms projecting out from the book! I gasped alerting the ladies who then questioned me.

"Tell us what you see?"

I put my glasses back on so I could see clearly but as I did, the holograms disappeared. I scrunched my brows together while confusion set in.

"We're waitingggggg," Director Pankins reminded me.

"I uh … I thought I saw something but I guess my eyes were just playing tricks on me."

Director Pankins pounded on her desk and looked hard into my eyes and said, "If you're lying, you will pay for it dearly, do you understand?"

"Hey, cool down. She's just a child." Miss Judge looked at me while talking to Miss Pankins.

After a devilish glare in my direction, the director stated, "We're not done with you yet, but you may leave for now."

"Who me?" I asked.

"Who else?" she impatiently asked while spreading her arms around to indicate that I was the only other person that should be skedaddling from her office.

"Oh, okay," I said as I stood up to leave.

Miss Judge gave me a reassuring side smile while I made my exit. Miss Place was impatiently waiting for me in the hallway. Director Pankins called out to Miss Place saying, "Take her to Miss Treetment would you, I think she has conjunctivitis."

Conjuntiv-i-what? I wondered. What was she talking about?

"How repulsive." Miss Place looked at my eye with pure disgust. I must have looked hideous. I bowed my head feeling shameful for whatever putrid disease I had.

CHAPTER 16
Some Things Need Shaking

After Holly left, the director was coming undone. "She knows something! She's just not telling us!" she roared.

"Well, with you behaving this way … yelling at her and being impatient is not helping at all! Who would want to help you?" Willow scolded the director. "I certainly wouldn't."

"I saw something last night that was unbelievable. I was hoping to see if she had changed."

"What did you see?"

The director pictured the spectacular show where Holly was washed in a cascade of stars but decided not to speak of it. Instead she changed the subject to her real purpose. "She's too comfortable here. We need to shake things up." Director Pankins paced the room racking her brain. "Maybe it's her sister being here. It's never a good idea for them to be too comfortable."

"Who would ever say that this place was too comfortable?" Willow said while gesturing toward all the strangeness that characterized this house.

It may have been a coincidence, but it could not have been both of their imaginations working in unison when the windows and floors shuddered after Willow's implication. It was as if the house itself was listening to their conversation and had something to add. The ladies braced themselves, looked at one another, but said nothing. Their eyes, however, communicated silently. After a while, Willow walked to the window and peered outside to see if anything could have caused such a raucous.

Miss Pankins went back to pacing across the wooden floors but became still when she came within the frame of her mirror. She was not moving, but something within the glass vibrated. She reached out her hand to steady it when the mirror stopped moving on its own. However, her reflection was missing.

Afraid of looking like a madwoman, she ignored the irregularity while the irony of her sister's sentiments rang through Director Pankins' ears.

"Strange indeed," the director seeped.

CHAPTER 17
Poop Eye

Miss Place knocked on Miss Treetment's door then stepped in without an invitation. Miss Treetment was busy painting her toenails green which were overgrown and curled over the edges. The moldy color enhanced the fungal look. She slowly twisted the nail polish stick back onto the bottle. With her big red lips curled into a circle, she blew on her wet toes. She wasn't in a hurry to address her patient—me.

"The director says this nitwit has pink eye," Miss Place scoffed.

"Pink guy?" Miss Treetment teased.

"Ha ha … no, pink *EYE*." The ladies shared a quick fake laugh.

"Pink eye? I thought she said, con-junk-ta-vi-tusk," I said, not quite getting the joke.

She put her hand on her hip and gave me a look that said, *you poor stupid dumb ugly infectious girl.*

I looked back at her unsure if her assessment was untrue. Maybe *I was a poor stupid dumb ugly infectious girl.*

"It's the same thing, dear, but c'mon, let's have look," Miss Treetment signaled for me to come closer to her. I guess she didn't want to get up, possibly wrecking her nails.

She took off my glasses and set them aside. Her wide face became a little blurry, but I could see her big eyes magnified by her thick glasses moving side to side while she inspected my peepers.

"I think it's this clumpy eyelash that could be causing all this redness. Let me just get a cotton swab and snatch that rascal out," she said before she swiped my eye. "But just to be on the safe side, I'll give her a hot compress to draw out any infection. You can leave her with me; this may take a while."

Miss Place left the office after saying that she'd be back for me in one hour. Miss Treetment heated up a rag and told me to press it on my eye. At first it was so hot, it practically burned my eyelid. But after some time, it cooled off, then she warmed it back up again over and over.

After my healing regimen, Miss Treetment walked over to take the rag. In her other hand, at the tip of her finger, she held my eyelash. "Want to make a wish?" she asked. I looked up confused at first then remembered that if I blew away my eyelash, I could make a wish. I closed my eyes and wished that I could see Falafel again, just once. I blew extra hard concentrating on my request. After I opened them, Miss Treetment nodded while offering me a sly side smile. I felt a tad better until Miss Place came back and looked me over, still obviously grossed out.

I went back to my room utterly befuddled—not from the confrontation with Miss Judge and Director Pankins, my pink eye, or my lash wish. I was perplexed and dazzled by the quick glimpse I had caught within the pages of the book, *Sage Themes*. Were my eyes playing tricks on me or did I actually see an image project out from the page? It didn't just sit there stagnant like a pop-up book that as a baby I had enjoyed countless times. The images were in motion as if they were living. I recalled the basic shapes—I saw what looked like a blacked-out sun with a glowing rim amidst intersecting lines in the shape of a cross, a beam of light hitting a mirror, an explosion, then crops blowing in the wind, but it all flashed by so quickly. Speaking of crops blowing—I really had to go to the bathroom.

All those images and details I was trying to conjure were replaced with echoing gasps and "Oh my goshes".

"What's wrong with your eyes?" Camellia asked as we were washing our hands in front of the mirror. I looked at myself and saw the redness from the hot compress still evident around my eye.

"Looks like pink eye," she said and all the girls gasped.

"No, it's con-junk-ta-vi-tusk," I stated trying to sound more sophisticated.

"It's pronounced *con-junc-tiv-i-tis* and it's the same thing as pink eye," Camellia said.

"I heard it's from wiping poop in your eye," another girl said.

"Ew, you wiped poop in your eye?" a bunch of girls asked.

"NO!!!" I said. "Who wipes poop in their eye?"

"Looks like you *do do*!" another girl chimed in, and they all started laughing at me.

I decided to leave the bathroom before anyone else could make more jabs at my eyes. I made a beeline for the dining hall overhearing other groups of kids mumbling. I imagined they were discussing my putrid pink eye situation.

Along the way, the twins each gallantly grabbed one of my arms then tucked them into their elbows. "Me lady, we'll be escorting you to the dining hall, if it pleases you," Staniel said in an attempt at formality.

I giggled at the gesture, nevertheless allowing them to lead me to the dining hall. A voice from behind screamed, "She's got pink eye!" The twins promptly dropped both of my arms. *So* … I walked into the dining hall without my formal escorts. I *knew* everyone was talking about me.

One by one, all of my friends except Begonia sat shoving various, barely edible, foods into their mouths while talking and spitting chunks onto their trays until the feeling of fullness was found.

"You don't look like you have pink eye," Danley said as he nibbled at his food.

"It was just an eyelash."

"That's what Danley always says when I catch him crying during a sad movie," Staniel teased.

"Staniel's too busy watching me to see if I'm crying to actually get moved by a thought-provoking motion picture," Danley maturely stated.

In order to set the record straight, I ignored their bickering and said, "I didn't really have pink eye. Miss Treetment just did a hot compress *in case* I had it. My eyes were just a little crusty from an eyelash, that's all."

"Let me have a look," Juniper came over and gave me a closer inspection.

I was tired of these eye examinations from everyone. I wished that the conversation would just get dropped, already.

"Can everyone please stop talking about my eye?" I pleaded.

"Sorry Holly, just letting you know that I think you're okay," Juniper said.

"I know I'm okay! Geeeeez! Just leave me be," I huffed.

Everyone backed off, thankfully. I wanted to think about something more exciting and less disgusting. I tried to reset my thoughts while I slowly chewed on an apple. Where was Begonia? I wondered. She was probably getting Dookie some food, I thought. Little Dookie, he was such a sweet little hammy ham hamster. Then out of nowhere, my brain pictured the amazing events I had witnessed the previous evening.

I had this crazy thing happen to me, I wanted to say but wasn't sure what crazy story I should share. I thought about the stars falling and the ground streaming with swimming lights. I thought about how I had glowed and made light trails. It all sounded too wondrous to be true. Would they even believe me?

"What happened, Holly?" Déjeuner asked.

"Huh?" I asked.

"You said that you had this crazy thing happen to you."

"I said that out loud?"

"Well, it wasn't *that* loud, but, yes, I heard you say it."

"I didn't hear her say anything," Staniel said.

"Me neither and we're sitting right next to her and you're way over there," Danley affirmed while pointing across the table.

I was confused. *What's going on?*

"I don't know," Déjeuner said.

"Can you hear my thoughts?" I asked thinking that it just wasn't possible.

"I don't know if it's possible or not, but you keep talking and I keep hearing," Déjeuner said with a shrug. "Are you gonna tell me what happened or not?"

I scanned everyone's bewildered faces. Juniper looked like she had a whole apple on the inside of one of her cheeks—not being crunched. Clover stared at Déjeuner who nibbled on a biscuit like a little mouse. Staniel and Danley shared a yawn as I came to the possibility that along with Déjeuner's other heightened senses, perhaps she could also hear my thoughts.

I wondered if it had anything to do with the stars falling.

"Stars falling? What happened?" Déjeuner asked.

I started to tell everyone about what happened but before I could, Coriander came in and told me to get up, "Quickly!" he ordered.

I stood then followed him after I scooted my chair under the table and put my tray away. I looked back at the twins who shook their heads like they were second fiddle. I put my hands up trying to explain, but Coriander grabbed my arm hurrying me along. I heard all their chairs move around figuring that they weren't going to let any secret action take place without them getting involved. I was right because I saw them trying to be sneaky while following us.

"What's going on?" I asked while trying to keep up with Coriander as he led the way. I was practically jogging to keep up when I saw Begonia and those two dipsticks, Thistle and Nettle, with three ugly boys huddled near the theater giggling. One boy with wet-looking lips scooted up closer to Begonia who didn't scoot away. Instead she gave him a playful smile.

Ewwww.

I didn't like the looks of that situation but I had no time to stop and question nor did I really want to because of the sneers Thistle and Nettle both directed my way as we passed.

"You are never going to believe this, even if I told you," Coriander said with excitement.

I shook my head trying to clear out the unfortunate sight I had just walked past. I followed him, running through the gigantic house, down the stairs, and outside. We ran around back toward the place where the ground had been covered in a star shower.

I saw something that wasn't there before. It must have popped up overnight. How was this possible? What was I seeing? I stopped for a minute to make sure my vision was not being distorted by my glasses again. I took them off and saw a fully forming, gorgeous, cosmic-colored growing garden! I put my glasses back on to make sure it was still there. Yup, this thing … this strangely-formed, colored garden was still there. But was it real?

CHAPTER 18

UNBELIEVABLE EYES

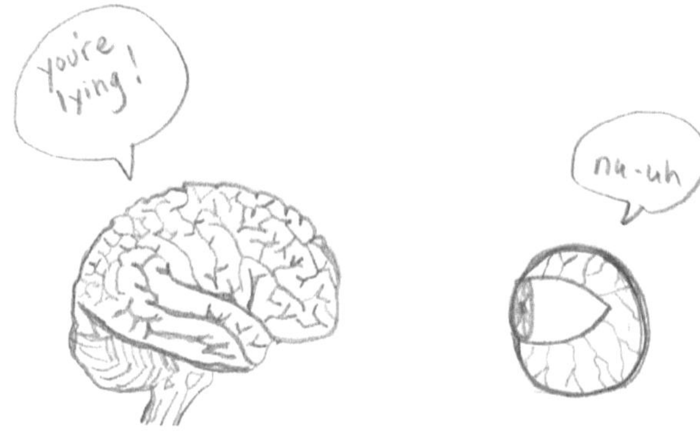

I couldn't believe my eyes! They had been playing too many tricks on me recently. I would have to rely on Coriander to make sure that what I saw was real. The garden was literally growing before our eyes. It was nearly bigger than the glowing garden that had once taken up this space.

A swirling kaleidoscope made from the same essence of miracles displayed itself before me. I could see each enchanted tree and spectral shrub gaining more and more colorful foliage, greenery, flowers, and girth. But the shapes and colors that were forming were not typical earth tones; the plants were made with an out-of-this world palette—colors of the cosmos—similar to some of the pictures

Miss Guide had shown us of star births, nebulas, and other galactic events. These hues were more vivid yet less imposing than the colors that were familiar to me. The rainbow spectrum was replaced with something ethereal and more celestial. A humming or buzzing tone suggested resurgence with its electrical pulses. Maybe it was the sound of life forming and growing.

This growing garden could grow bigger than The Children's Horrible House itself. When I looked over at the house, I had to do a double take … the house had taken on a new reflective metallic shade. What was happening?

"Oh my goodness, Coriander, what has happened?"

"I have no idea."

"Whoa!!! This place is crazy!" the twins said, unable to hide anymore.

Coriander turned around to see everyone standing with looks of awe and wonder. Their marveling was understandable and warranted. As well, Déjeuner echoed everyone's feelings as she placed her hands on the tendrils of an unearthly plant reaching down to her.

We stood together within a place that had intersected with another world, outside of our atmosphere. All of the changes that were appearing before us must have had something to do with the falling stars. Maybe those stars were seeds from outer space that implanted themselves into the ground. The rain that came down could have caused them to grow while washing The Children's Horrible House in this supernatural hue. I don't really know, but after I thought about the other night's events, I came up with no other conclusion.

"It's not exactly The Children's Horrible Garden that the director planned, but sometimes plans don't go the way we expect," Coriander said in a ripened tone.

We walked within the garden which had an order to it like I had never seen. Instead of it being a maze, it had spirals like a hurricane or a galaxy that slowly swirled continuously while forming the garden! Each tunnel led to the center where the tomb of Hawthorne North Star still stood, unburned by the fire that had torched the rest of the glowing garden.

I heard a rustling coming from behind the stone building. I immediately jumped behind Coriander who stood steadfast. There it went again, this time more rustling, then a whoosh of air flapped beneath the wings of glowing birds that looked like they had descended from heaven. A flock of iridescent doves emerged from who knows where, claiming their command station around the tomb of Hawthorne North Star. They made a series of song-like coos while they strutted. Just like everything in this garden, they, too, appeared supernatural.

"I wonder where they came from?"

"Looks like they came from heaven," Juniper said with her younger angel-like voice.

It was obvious enough, some sort of extra-terrestrial event took place. The star drops that I had witnessed were not just a dream. It actually happened before my eyes. Perhaps parts of heaven did fall, implanting their essence into the earth, transforming it into something out of this world. Even the scent that overwhelmed my nostrils was filled with something that induced wonderment and excitement—like Christmas Eve—cookies, milk, and magic.

We walked silently for some time within the garden which could only be described as miraculous. I remember the first and other times I had strolled through the glowing garden and saw that it was magnificent, but this—this was what people could die for. If I had died and saw this,

I would never want to live again as long as I could stay here.

"You guys, I'm in awe. I don't think I've ever seen a place in my most stretched imagination that could compete with this place's … everything," I marveled.

"I would have to agree with you. I wonder what made this happen?" Coriander asked.

"I could tell you, but you probably wouldn't believe me."

"Yeah?" he said obliviously.

"Honestly, it was pretty unbelievable, and I probably wouldn't believe it if I didn't witness it with my own eyes."

"Uh huh …"

I got the feeling that Coriander wasn't listening to me. He was just saying unnecessary words like *yeah* and *uh huh* pretending to appease me, so I repeated my last sentence to see if he was actually listening.

"Honestly, it was pretty unbelievable, and I probably wouldn't believe it if I didn't witness it with my own eyes."

He looked at me after my repetitious words finally sank in and asked, "What are you talking about?"

"Tell us already!" Clover prodded.

I took a breath, not quite ready to go over the other night's episode but then decided that because Coriander and everyone else understood the craziness that we had encountered here at The Children's Horrible House, I could probably count on them to comprehend the night I saw drops of heaven fall.

I told them, and they listened with excitement and shock at my carefully detailed retelling. They asked me for more specifics. While I obliged, they replied with a lot of *wows* and *holy molies*. But I could tell they weren't just empty exclamations.

"But why? What's the reason?" Coriander skeptically asked, thinking that it couldn't just be a random miracle.

I shrugged and thought about something. "You know what this means, right?"

"What?" Clover asked.

"That new garden that we were going to have to plant in order for us to get to go to the Star Day celebration? The Evening of Enchantment? Or whatever it's called … It's done! And we didn't have to lift a finger!" Danley said excitedly.

"He speaketh the truth!" Staniel said in his made-up formal tone.

While I anticipated the fun we would have on Star Day, my eyes rested on the tomb of Hawthorne North Star, and if I hadn't already seen unbelievable things, I wouldn't believe that I saw a sparkle twinkle from the "O" in his middle name.

"Did you see that?" I asked.

"I did!" Coriander exclaimed. "But I thought it was my overactive imagination."

We bolted over to the stone and touched the letters. I hadn't noticed an etching of a nautical star carved out around the letter before. By sheer curiosity, I peeked into the "O" and saw an eyeball staring back at me. I jumped back.

"What?" Clover asked wondering what took me by surprise.

"Um, see for yourself …" I must have looked accosted because only Coriander hesitantly looked into the hole.

"What did you see?" he asked after peering inside the peephole.

"Did you *not* see the eyeball?"

He looked again, "Nope."

I peeked inside, and this time saw what must be the inside

of the mausoleum. Who was inside there? I tried to see if I could find anyone in the corners but nothing or no one stirred … or so I thought.

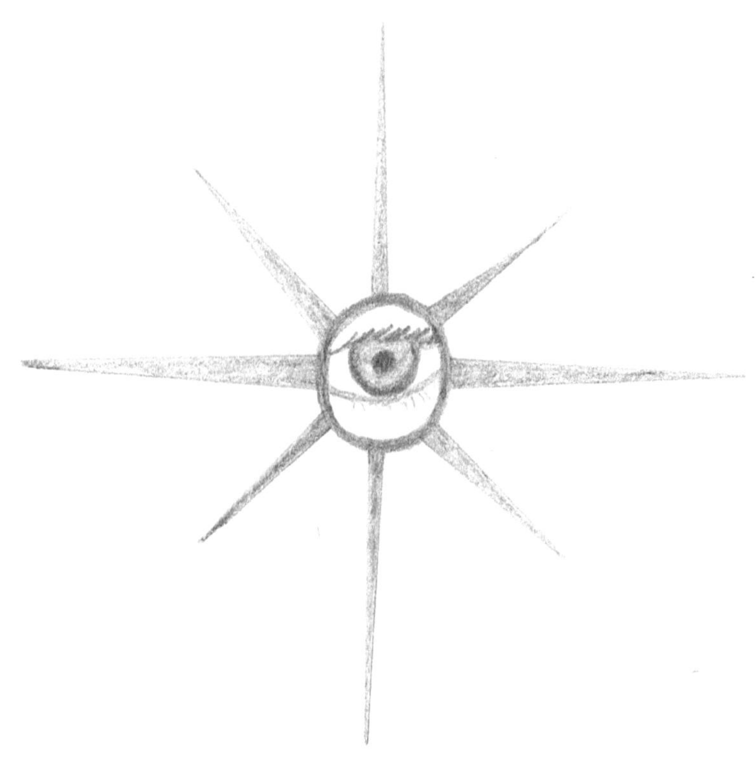

CHAPTER 19
Something's Wrong

While Juniper was making beds one morning, Miss Place came in and escorted her to Director Pankins' office. Juniper stood obediently while the director informed her of her new plans.

"You've completed the program … I should add … once again." The director pretended to congratulate Juniper with a strained smile. "Now you may return home." To most pupils, this was exactly what they hoped to hear.

Juniper was confused. Why was the director acting so strangely? But then, what was *normal* for Director Pankins?

"Huh?" Juniper was buying time.

"Here is your certificate of completion." The director handed Juniper a formal ribbon-wrapped scroll. "I'm sure your parents will be very proud."

"But … what if I'm not ready to go home yet?"

Out of some sort of kindness, Director Pankins paused to think but never answered her. Instead of punishing Juniper for her insolence, she instructed Major Whoopins and Mr. Ree to return Juniper to her home.

"Wait! I need to get Holly. I'll go, but I need to take her with me. I came here to bring her home."

The director promptly said, "I see."

"I won't leave here without my sister," Juniper insisted.

"Yes … yes … Gentlemen, you know what to do," the director said before she stepped out of her office.

"C'mon Punkin', we don't want no trouble." Major Whoopins tried to calm Juniper down after seeing panic invade her face.

"I won't leave here without my sister. *DO YOU UNDERSTAND ME?*" Juniper was much older than the other kids who filled the halls and chambers of The Children's Horrible House. Mr. Ree and Major Whoopins would have to be very tactful about this.

"Don't worry, Sparky, we will get Holly on our way out." Mr. Ree used coaxing terms of endearment to calm her. He looked at Major Whoopins hoping to sound just as convincing.

Juniper wanted to believe them because she really couldn't wait to go home but she wouldn't leave without Holly.

"Do you promise?" she asked.

"Without a doubt, Punkin'," Major Whoopins said.

"You have nothing to worry about, Sparkles," Mr. Ree joined in knowing that their attempts to put her at ease were becoming excessive and flat out incredulous.

The three of them walked from the director's office toward the dormitories. They passed the twins and Déjeuner who immediately sensed something wrong in the situation.

"Where are they taking you?" Déjeuner asked.

"Oh! Déjeuner …" Juniper began but was cut off.

"No talking! 'Less ya'll want some DUNGEON time!" Major Whoopins dropped his sweetness and used his booming voice to stop any more chatter.

Juniper didn't want Déjeuner to get into trouble on her account so she said, "It's okay Déjeuner, don't worry. I'm just looking for Holly, then I'll be right back."

Déjeuner wasn't buying it. Her instincts were too powerful and precise for her to ignore, but getting locked up in THE DUNGEON wouldn't be helpful in any way for Juniper. Both boys gave Déjeuner a nudge for her to go with them. She followed until they found Clover who was coming from bed-making duty.

"Something's wrong," the twins said to Clover.

"Duh … what's right in this place?"

"No, we're serious; something's going on with Juniper."

"What is it?"

"We don't know."

"Well, you guys are just … well … just … I don't know, full of nothin'."

"Full of nothing? That doesn't make any sense," Staniel scrunched his nose and eyebrows.

"Oh … because you guys are makin' all kinds a sense," Clover sarcastically stated when she decided to leave the conversation.

Déjeuner spoke up and said, "They may not make any sense, but they're right about Juniper, something's going on, and it doesn't feel right."

A worried expression instantly spread over Clover's face. "What should we do?" she asked.

"Let's find Holly," the twins said in unison.

They walked together until they ran into Thistle, Nettle, and

Begonia. The twins instinctually knew that this was a bad-people combo but cast those thoughts aside to keep to the task at hand.

"Hey Begonia, have you seen Holly?" Danley asked.

"*Hey Begonia, have you theen Holly*?" Thistle and Nettle mimicked with dopey facial expressions.

The twins gave the two girls a look of boredom before turning to Begonia with a gesture that suggested, *is this the kind of people you're hanging around with now*?

Clover spoke up, "Hey! He didn't ask *you*. He asked *her*." She pointed to Begonia.

"Who are you talking to? Becauth your one eye ith looking over here, and your other eye ith looking over there," Thistle meanly exaggerated.

"That's real funny coming from someone who spits every time they speak," Staniel said, sticking up for Clover and his twin.

Déjeuner cut through the insults and asked again, "Begonia, have you seen Holly?"

Begonia's demeanor warmed as she replied, "I haven't seen Holly, but if I do, I'll tell her that you are looking for her."

Thistle and Nettle looked at each other and then at Begonia. They whispered to one another then issued an ultimatum, "Ith either usth or them … you dethide."

Begonia looked like a trapped bunny but stayed quiet while the rest of her true friends walked away.

CHAPTER 20
A Walk Within a Greedy Garden

Director Pankins was walking toward the library. As she was about to open the door, Reed Trustworthy put his hand on it, keeping it closed. She wasn't expecting this interruption. However, she was never expecting the run-ins she had with Reed. Though they were mostly inconvenient, these encounters weren't as uncomfortable as she had anticipated.

"Let's take a little walk outside, shall we?" Reed intercepted Sirius and escorted her downstairs.

She went along silently, listening to his uneven breaths as his pace quickened. He was a regal man even in his diminutive role as a servant to her father and her family. Although time had imposed character lines on his face and punctuated his hair with silver linings, he kept his stature and strength throughout the years. Every time she regarded Reed, she was reminded of her childhood, how he had played with her when no one else was around, tucked her in at night when her father was too busy, and brought her silly special treats like roly-polies or cocoons. A soft spot had developed for him and had never totally hardened.

As she stepped outside, the air warmed her skin and freshened her lungs. Scents from the garden slithered from its source reaching beyond its boundaries. In the distance she spotted something stretching out from where dust and dirt once lay. What happened? Was her garden whole again? As she came closer, she realized that it was not her garden but rather something much more supernatural.

As they approached, spirals of exceptional beauty reached out for her; she hesitated. A presence within the garden attracted her, yet at the same time, made her fearful. She felt it when she peripherally looked upon it from her vantage. She wasn't surprised by this garden's phantasmagoric appearance nor its vibration which echoed from the ground. What surprised her was that she had absently stared at it from her perch and didn't realize it was so wildly different from the garden that had been destroyed—her glowing garden. Had she completely missed the impetus to this massive mythical growing garden? Or, *wait a minute*, she thought. She *had* seen its beginning, the night the stars fell on and all around Holly Spinatsch.

That night produced a feeling she would hope to repress. She had never felt so inadequate—like she had missed a blessing meant for her, it'd been passed on to someone so obviously less worthy. Her selfish thoughts stalled when Reed's words intersected them.

"I have a feeling that this is a sign," Reed began. "Actually, I can't even justifiably use that term. Well, I don't know what to call this," he said while raising his arms and signaling all the glory that surrounded them, "but what you've been waiting for is about to happen," he said with surety.

"What?" she asked.

He wasn't sure if or how exactly to answer her question. He continued to walk deeper into the garden. It grew thicker and more abundant with each step. The flowers, stems, and foliage held a pulsing light from within that appeared to be radioactive or, more appropriately, characterized as otherworldly—indescribable.

Sirius tried to get more information from Reed while feeling strange sensations all around herself. A cooing sound grew around them as doves roosted around Hawthorne North Star's mausoleum.

Reed studied the bewildering birds and shook his head in wonderment. "The signs are all around us."

"I know I wanted the children to help build a new garden, but this just happened on its own. I, sadly, had nothing to do with this …" Sirius said, perplexed by his apparent mission.

"Don't always act so coy. I know what you're after. But *you* must be careful. I was hoping it wouldn't come to this, but you may just get a lot more than what you think you want."

"You're telling me to not be so coy; I find your diffidence to be quite humorous," Sirius said as she felt something tickling her neck. Absently, she swiped whatever it was away.

"I'm funny, yes, I know," Reed said flatly, "but I need to warn the both of you to be careful. What you're playing with could cause irreparable loss."

"You make no sense sometimes. *The both of you*?" Sirius said while stalking further into the creeping, growing garden.

"You and Willow are trying to find something that you think belongs to you, right?"

Sirius ignored his question while walking further then stopped and stared at a curious cluster of blooms. In an instant she was caught in a swirling trance. A flower slowly opened into a giant ferocious-looking snap dragon that jolted from its stem and almost engulfed her face. She jumped back before she felt a grip take hold of her arm. "Take your hands off me!" She turned ready to smack Reed when she saw a vexing vine twisting around her arms. More pulchritudinous vines found her ankles and were climbing up her legs. Sirius screamed. Instantly her mouth was silenced by the voracious creeper. She shook her head, arms, and legs trying to get the vines to come loose, but they were too strong for her. She writhed and wriggled to no avail. The tendrils grew more savage as they were twisting and turning trying to pull her into the fullness of its spiraling tentacles until Reed finally stepped in. He tugged, broke, and kicked the vines. They were relentless, but he was even more aggressive as he went into a blind rage until she was set free.

Once he pried her from the smothering invasive garden, they ran. The garden growled while growing around them making their escape route continuous. The plants were younger and therefore weaker at the garden's edges. Smaller, less mordacious vines and bushes tried to cling to her as they staggered from the garden.

After they were securely out from the reaches of the aggressive vines, Sirius held onto Reed much like she had as a child, allowing him to lead her to a safe place where nothing could harm her. The trust that had been earned many years ago was not lost, but not yet fully reestablished.

"What is wrong with this horrible place?" she asked out of breath.

"This place … this garden is beautiful but, yes, horribly dangerous." Then Reed mumbled something that she couldn't understand.

"What did you say?" Sirius asked with her fiery eyes reflecting fear.

"Oh, nothing …"

"Please tell me," she said with an inkling of her youthful voice that he could never resist. She was the closest thing to what could be his own child. He couldn't help but think of her like that.

He stopped walking then turned to her. He looked into her mother's, Sings-in-the-Meadow's, spitting image and quietly uttered, "I said, 'like you'."

Her scared face became confused. "Like me, what?"

"The garden is beautiful but very dangerous … like you."

Sirius couldn't argue with him about that, but she could regain her composure. She stood up after straightening out her clothes and hair.

"I think I need to rest. Would you mind helping me back to my room?" she asked.

Steadily, Reed led Sirius Pankins back to her room. She sat down in her chair and Reed turned to leave, but before he could go, Sirius said, "As the old saying goes, be careful what you wish for, right?"

Reed nodded, unsure of which wish she was referring to.

"It really is a *horrible* garden," she said.

CHAPTER 21
Reflections

Willow, entered the room while dusk was settling into the sky. Pomegranate rays brightened the usually smothered grey walls. But as the sun set, so did the temporary warmth, leaving the room in its ordinary dreary doldrums. In the director's office, Willow was searching for the book that Holly had been asked to study a few days earlier. She had seen a glimmer of surprise in Holly's gaze. But what had Holly seen? Willow thumbed through the same book, but nothing jumped out at her, as it clearly had for Holly. After looking and relooking, she closed it a tad harder than she had planned.

She slumped over the desk, dismayed by not learning anything new. She picked up *The Message*, after being let down by *Sage Themes*. She was reading over the histories and lineages when something caught the corner of her eye. It was a flash coming from the mirror that hung on the wall. She turned and looked at the mirror and noticed a plaque that was in the reflection. It read in a strange-looking slant,

When Willow turned to read the plaque with her own eyes–not in the reflection, it read:

Knowing yourself is the beginning of all wisdom.

-Aristotle

She blinked, making sure she wasn't seeing things and regarded the plaque again from each angle. Out of some strange intuition, she stood up while holding the book and held it before the mirror. With a look of astonishment on her face, she stared at the hidden message within the book when the door creaked open.

Willow jumped and slammed the book shut before her delayed scream echoed throughout the house.

"What is it?" Director Pankins demanded, clearly shaken by the librarian's outburst.

Reed Trustworthy rushed in, ready to rescue the women from danger. When he saw that no actual danger lurked, he let down his guard. The same could not be said for Miss Pankins.

"What are you doing in here?" she asked, suspicious of Willow's intentions.

Knowing that there was no way to explain herself out of this situation, Willow came clean and explained, "I was trying to figure out what Holly Spinatsch could have seen when she looked in the book. At first, I couldn't figure it out, but when I was examining this book, something caught my eye. Actually, a flash from the mirror caught my eye, and, by mere chance, I held *The Message* up to the mirror and I saw it."

"What did you see?" the director prodded.

"The real message … look, see for yourself."

Reed stood unflinchingly as if he already knew this information. Director Pankins felt his deception.

"You knew this already, didn't you?" Sirius accused while walking past him.

Reed looked away.

"Come see," Willow urged while she stood in front of the mirror in Sirius' office.

Willow held the book up to the mirror, and, suddenly, instead of seeing small letters, drawings, and other ramblings, large letters projected from the pages of the book. But they were just letters, all about the same size, with the same amount of spaces between them. The font was oversized, strange, root-like, and tendril-y-scroll-ish—like the vines that had tried to capture Sirius Pankins. Sirius caught a chill that ran down her spine like a telepathic vine strangling. It gave her the heebie-jeebies so much that she had to look away.

Each page that Willow turned held more letters. She mouthed out their identities as if they would somehow turn into a sentence that would, hopefully, eventually make sense.

Sirius shook off her fear and remembered that she was in the safety of her office. She flipped through the pages then stood back looking in the mirror, hoping that they might make some sense to her. She flipped again and again and slowly became agitated.

It was Reed's turn to roll his eyes.

"What do these letters mean?" Miss Pankins asked Reed.

"If I told you, then what fun would that be?" Reed said while his left eyebrow rose as well as some blood into his normally stony face.

"You don't know, do you?" she implied.

"I don't need to prove anything to you. You, however, have only proven to be pigheaded, selfish, and unworthy."

Sirius had trouble thinking that Reed was still hung up on their past. But she had no time to rehash their conflict. In an attempt to get things moving, she tried to give him what he wanted from her.

"Okay, yes … I was wrong. I shouldn't have betrayed you. But honestly, I didn't think I was. I did what was required. I finished my schooling, I was obedient, and if it weren't for *your death*, maybe things would have turned out differently," she said with a little more emotion around the word *death* than she had planned.

Reed changed his face from calculating to thoughtful.

"I think it's either one long sentence or a word game," Willow said as if the conversation Reed and Sirius were exchanging was not happening. "Let's start from the beginning. Write down each letter as I read it to you."

Sirius grabbed a pencil and paper and wrote down each letter. This took some time. After at least an hour, Reed was intrigued and amused by the two of them working together. He watched while flashes of Saffron as a child became visible in the director's expressions while focused on her task. And though he hadn't been close to Willow as a child, he saw the familiar resemblance of her mother, and it brought him back to much more secure and happy times. He missed his so-called family that he had in The North Star residence. He missed Hawthorne and Sings-in-the-Meadow horribly. Then he blurted out something that stunned them and him.

"They're not dead."

CHAPTER 22
Ketchup Farts

Coriander and I walked from our afternoon classes to get something to eat for dinner. I was starving. My stomach had been extra hungry lately. It was like I couldn't eat enough food. I wanted everything they served just to shut my stomach up.

"Are you going to finish that?" I asked Coriander who seemed less interested in his tray.

"For real? You *want* to eat this stuff?"

"Yes! I'm still hungry!"

"Go ahead," he said when he gave me access to his overcooked carrots, brown spinach, mushy applesauce, and mysterious bubbly purple meat.

"All it needs is a sprinkle of taste enhancement," I said.

"What's that?"

"Taste enhancement? Don't you know? Meet my delicious friends, salt and ketchup, they make all this slop a little yummier." I sprinkled a dash of salt over everything before squeezing fart noises from the ketchup bottle.

I couldn't help but giggle. Farts from any source made me laugh even if they did not go well with the thought of food. I pecked, gobbled, and shoved the grub down like a vulture while Coriander looked disgusted.

"I have to go now," he said as he stood up to leave.

"Why?" I muffled with my mouth overstuffed with food.

His face looked like he was about to get ill. He pointed at my open full mouth and said, "That's why."

"Why what?" I asked spilling out crumbs.

"And you make gross mouth noises. You sound like a cow chewing cud." His face and smile turned upside down in disgust at my engorgement.

"Sorry," I said after I stuffed more food inside my mouth.

I WAS HUNGRY!

Coriander tried to leave as quickly as possible. But not before he took my empty tray and got the *a-okay* from Miss Shapen who was making sure he wasn't being wasteful. *I* should have gotten two *a-okays* because *I* was the real un-wasteful one—not Coriander.

While I was chewing and thinking truly useless thoughts, the twins, Clover, and Déjeuner walked into the dining hall. After they spotted me, they almost galloped over to my table.

"Something's going on," the twins said in unison.

Just when they said this, Begonia walked in with Thistle, Nettle, and three dirty-looking, ugly boys. Begonia was holding the wet-lipped boy's hand.

Ew!

Where was Dookie? Begonia had taken it upon herself to be Dookie's guardian while we were here at The Children's Horrible House, and I had trusted her. But something had me unsettled.

"Are you listening to us?" the twins asked.

"Huh? Oh, I'm sorry. What did you say?"

"Something's going on, we said."

"As usual," I answered the twins with little reaction to their statement. All I wanted to know right now was Dookie's whereabouts.

"Something's going on with Juniper," Déjeuner clarified.

"Juniper? What? What's going on?" I asked, suspending my thoughts on Begonia and Dookie.

"We don't know."

"O … kay," I said confused by their information which was not exactly informative.

They started to talk all at once, making everything they were saying sound like blubbering mumbles. I wiped my mouth then organized my tray when they shushed each other and decided to let Déjeuner speak for them.

"Major Whoopins and Mr. Ree were taking her somewhere, but I could sense that something wasn't right. I didn't know for sure; I just had this feeling."

"Where were they taking her?" I asked.

"Not sure but I think we should go look for her."

Without a second thought, I jolted out of my seat, and we set out to find Juniper. We looked in the classrooms, the library, the theater, THE DUNGEON, the bathrooms, the everything else rooms, and still, no sign of Juniper. But I did find Dookie in a make-shift cage next to Begonia's bottom bunk. He was eating some lettuce. I gave him a pet before picking him up and taking his whole cage back to my room. Since Begonia had no time for Dookie, I would take him back with me.

I set his cage up on the windowsill so he could look outside while doing his hamster activities. After I had Dookie all arranged, I went back to Clover, Déjeuner, and the twins in the hallway who were still trying to figure out where Juniper could be.

"Where could she be?" Clover asked.

"Let's look outside, maybe?" Staniel said.

"Good idea," I said.

From behind, an old crackly voice that didn't belong to any of us asked, "You know what's an even better idea?"

We turned and saw mean old Mr. Meanor standing like an overgrown troll. Thistle and Nettle sauntered past while making disgusted faces at me. I had no time for their antics. "You pesky kids need to get back to work."

We looked around at the other kids who were shuffling back to bed-making duties knowing that we had to go make beds also. We stood not moving a tad too long, so Mr. Meanor prodded us like cattle until we were in our corral—where we dutifully made beds … again and again and again.

I wondered why Begonia wasn't with those two knuckleheads. If she wasn't hanging with them, who was she with? That ugly wet-lipped boy? *Yuck!*

The only thing that took my mind to a less annoyed state was the song that echoed throughout the house.

The Children's Horrible House
The Children's Horrible House
Where you eat gross food
that's never ever good.
The Children's Horrible House … Yuck …

I could hear the individual voices, some good, others less good, but I think that they added to the overall dark and dreary essence of the song. The tone itself held some kind of power of its own. It sort of put us in a trance—where we didn't care to think—as if we were robots under an orchestrated mind control.

Where you wake up at dawn
and always always yawn …
The Children's Horrible House … (Yawn noises)

The day was dragging, as were our efforts. You could tell that we were coming to the end by the direction each verse went.

Where you have to make your bed
and then sleep instead …

We sang along with whomever made something up while folding, flattening, and fluffing our afternoon away to the dramatic tune of … *The Children's Horrible House.*

CHAPTER 23
VAGUE CONCLUSIONS

Both Miss Judge and Director Pankins stood still like deer in headlights. Their eyes also appeared doe-like at the possibility of what Reed Trustworthy was suggesting. His words struck them like a car driving on an unlit road in the middle of nowhere. They were speechless—they looked at one another and then back to Reed.

"Who?" they asked, even though they suspected who he was referring to.

"You know who."

"How?" Willow asked.

"That's much more difficult to answer."

"You mean to tell me that our parents and family are still alive?"

"Yes, well, not exactly, no."

"What do you mean?" Sirius Pankins said in her usual agitated tone.

"Some of them are still alive."

"Who?"

"Your parents."

"My mother and father are still alive?" Willow asked.

"Actually, I'm sorry … your mother is ... I'm not sure … I apologize for being so vague, but your father is not dead."

The sisters looked heartbroken, confused, and skeptical all at once. They stared at Reed as if he were a doctor explaining things in medical lingo, not layman's terms.

"I think you need to be more clear," the director insisted.

"I don't think I will be able to explain myself in a way you would understand. Unfortunately, you will have to wait and see for yourselves … when the time is right."

"When will that be?" Willow asked even though she had a hunch.

"You will have to figure that out for yourselves. I've already said too much."

"Is there more that you have not told us?"

"Yes … and well, you'll see."

CHAPTER 24
MAGNETISM

After everyone left her office, Sirius Pankins stared out of the window and watched as the monstrous garden slowly swirled, and by inches, grew more and more wicked. How could something so miraculous and beautiful be so scary and menacing? A lure attracted her within the hypnotic spirals suggesting a promise, but the last time she was within the garden, it had tried to eat her. She couldn't go alone—even though the compulsion to go inside it was becoming irresistible.

With a great deal of effort, she pulled away from the window and caught a glimpse of something in the mirror hanging on her wall. It was a twinkling of light and she walked over to it as it was fading away into the center of the antique mirror. She shook her head, looked again, but it was no longer visible.

"I need a nap," she told herself.

Along the way to her chamber, she passed Holly Spinatsch in the hallway. Their eyes locked.

"Have you seen my sister, Juniper?" Holly boldly asked.

Miss Pankins looked around and said in her most convincing voice, "No, not today." She began to walk away before Holly could stare longer. Out of curiosity, Miss Pankins turned back around; Holly's eyes were still set on her. Sirius Pankins planted her stance, pointing her constricted fiery eyes directly on the pupil; Holly dropped her glare then walked away, defeated.

Staring contests never ended in victory for anyone against Sirius Pankins.

CHAPTER 25
The Chamber

That evening everyone crawled into bed with tedious routines weighing them down. But after what was about to happen to me in the middle of this night, I would have welcomed that monotonous predictability any day, or night, for that matter.

There I was, in sweet dreamy slumber when a strange sound echoed through the walls, into my ears. My eyes bugged open. I sat up wondering if I was simply hearing things inside of my head. I looked around at everyone else as they were still conked out. I heard it again. It wasn't like the peacocks' cry; it was more of a haunting mewl. I dragged myself out of bed and scampered across the room. Before I peeked out of the doorway into the hall, I heard it again. So I followed its call. The sound took me to an area I had never explored. This room was so hidden within the house that we kids weren't even allowed to clean it.

I was in Miss Pankins personal wing, feeling a bizarre inkling that I should leave immediately. The hairs on my arms stood up. I rubbed them back down before I heard a scratching on the other side of the door at the end of the hall. At first I became stiff but resolved to be brave. I scrambled over to it, twisted the knob, and walked inside a blue moonlit bedroom.

It was Hawthorne North Star's personal chamber. It had been largely left untouched or so it appeared. It was as if time had stood still in this room the moment he had last left it. Walled in dark burled paneling, the solemn room felt rich but with an intimidating ghostly sophistication. A spotlight flicked on, blinding me. I covered my eyes.

"Who's there?" I whispered, but no one responded. I tried to peek around the glare, but the light was too bright. I heard scampering, falling objects, before something scurried away—then, the sounds of silence.

What was going on? Who had made those sounds? My question was answered when a cat jumped up onto the bed making a gurgling meow.

"Hey!" I was startled. "So, I guess you're the one making all this racket," I scolded the kitty with much appreciated relief that it wasn't some haunting ghost.

He blinked then licked himself until his eyes became lazy. He curled up into a cinnamon bun as if he was ready to nap. Well, at least *someone* was comfortable, I thought.

I turned to see my shadow within the spotlight. I couldn't tell if it was intentional or coincidence, but my shadow lined up perfectly with a series of silhouettes hanging on the wall. The oval-framed black profiles were dignified-looking where mine was, as you probably have guessed, goofy-looking.

I got up while watching my outline grow taller and more menacing. I swayed back and forth, briefly playing with my shadow. Animals appeared on my hands when I held up my arms. For a second, I forgot where I was and made shadow puppets on the wall. I made your classic dog barking, a bunny wiggling his nose, a kitty cat … I tried to think of something more original when, without warning, the light went out.

I used my shadow puppet hands to find a gas lantern on the bedside table. I struck a match to light the wick. After I blew out the match flame, I turned, tripped on something, and stumbled to the ground. I heard the cat jump down to run for cover.

"Ouch!" I cried after I stumbled. Whatever made me trip, caused me to stub my big toe. Boy, did it hurt. A while back when my family was camping I had cried when I had stubbed my toe; my Dad said he was going to call the "Toe Truck" to come take my toe to get fixed. It made me giggle because I knew that "Tow Trucks" took broken-down cars to get fixed, not toes … silly Dad.

After inspecting my wound, I decided that I would survive. I just needed to give it a second. My toe throbbed with its new heartbeat. As I looked to see what had caused me to trip, I saw a doll face down on the floor with its head broken off.

It was the same doll I had seen up in the attic when Coriander and I discovered the Star Family Tree. I picked up the doll parts in both of my hands. It had long black hair and moccasins to match. I tried to put the head back on, but it wouldn't go back. Inside the neck, I found a rolled-up piece of paper which I carefully removed.

I unrolled the thick yellowed scroll covered with a bunch of handwritten symbols that I could not translate. It looked like a lot of lower case p's, q's, and angles. But at the end it was signed, Momma.

I felt the layered texture of the paper, rolled it up, and stuck it back inside the doll. I wondered if I should leave it here or bring the doll with me to my room. I didn't have to think for long because just as I was contemplating, the door opened as Miss Place in her night bonnet and gown arrived to scold me until I was back in my bunk with no doll.

"You'll pay for your nosiness in the morning," she promised through a yawn.

CHAPTER 26
PUNISHING ONESELF

I could hardly sleep after the threat of misery that I was sure to face upon awakening. I dreaded the punishment that was promised. My run-in with the director in the hallway didn't make me any more confident, in fact, it worsened my chances. I wanted to hide but knew that if I hid, my punishment would be doubled. I flinched while I imagined my spankings.

Phantom punishments kept tricking me while I attempted to relax and sleep until I was awakened by nothing but normalcy. My morning was plagued by the terror that awaited me. I kept my eye out for Miss Place to escort me to THE DUNGEON, but she never came. In fact, I never got punished at all.

I was reminded of the time I had spilled red nail polish all over my parents' yellow bedspread. I accidentally broke a bottle of nail polish after I foolishly banged them together. When Ginger came in witnessing my crimes dripping down the sides of the linens, her eyes grew along with my guilt.

"Oh woo woo! You are going to be in *soooooo* much trouble! When Mom sees what you've done, she is going to kill you!" Ginger taunted.

"Please don't tell on me!" I begged.

"I don't have to tell on you. Mom will know you did this; you are going to be in so much trouble!"

"Please, Ginger, please!"

"Okay, I won't tell, but you better hide."

For once, it seemed like Ginger was on my side. I took her advice and even added extra caution by stashing the paddle where no one would find it. After I placed the long wooden spanker under sheets and heavy objects, I found a quiet spot for myself to hide in the attic. No one would ever find me!

Hours passed without anyone looking for me. My parents still weren't home. I could hardly take anymore hiding. I was getting tired and hungry after so long. All this hiding and no punishment was grueling. I really wanted to come out when I finally heard my mom and dad come home.

I was going to get it. I knew it; my dad was going to spank me, big time. Then I overheard Ginger rat me out! She told on me and said, "Look what Holly did, Mom. She was playing with the nail polish and broke one, spilling it all over your bedspread."

The treachery! The deceit! The tattle-tale! The whatever else! I couldn't believe Ginger told on me! But why? Of course Ginger told on me. She hated me! But then I heard my mom say in her cheerful bird-like voice, "Oh, it's okay, I've always disliked this bedspread. I'll just get a new one!"

If you could picture a face filled with blankness, resentment, and a small dose of relief, that would have been mine in that moment. Ginger's face was probably matching my expressions, with one exception, relief.

So, basically, in order to avoid certain punishment, I punished myself by being cooped up for hours when there was no actual punishment for my so-called crime. *Thanks Ginger.*

* * *

Instead of some arduous punishment from Miss Place, what did occur was a mind-blowing class with Miss Guide. She talked about the S.T.C.

"Does anyone know what that stands for?" she asked the class. "S.T.C. stands for the Space Time Continuum."

No one knew what that meant so everyone kept quiet.

"Anyone want to give a guess as to what that is?"

"It's where time continues in space," a smart-looking boy with glasses guessed.

"Kamut, I'm pretty sure that you may have been guessing, but you are not too far off," Miss Guide said, reassuring him of his hunch. He instantly put a cocky look on his face while he tugged on his coverall collars.

"The concept of time is a tricky thing to define, describe, or dissect. Does time actually exist? Or is it an intangible term used to decide intervals or units of periods passing into the past or future? Is time linear? When did time start? Does time have an end? Are there other times existing parallel to our time? Could you travel through time? These are all questions that one must ask in order to understand time. It's not something that a scientist can observe under a microscope, or even hold in your hand, so how do we know time exists?"

Everyone was quiet for a moment. The only thing I could hear were gears in the kids' heads becoming engaged in thought.

"Birthdays?" someone blurted from behind me.

"You probably have no idea how right you are, do you?" Miss Guide loved it when her students not only paid attention but came to their own, well-thought-out conclusions. "What unit of time do we use to calculate birthdays?"

The answer I thought of seemed too simple that it couldn't possibly be right.

"Years," she stated the obvious.

Fiddle sticks! I was going to say that but thought she was looking for something much more out of reach for my brain to know.

"To be more precise, 365 days, the time it takes for the Earth to make its full orbit around the Sun. And to be even more precise 365.25 days, which is why we have a leap year every four years. Ancient Egyptians figured out that in order to get an accurate measurement of a year, they had to locate and track the stars in the sky throughout the year. To be specific, they used Sirius, the Dog Star, to calculate the days in a year which in turn predicted the annual Nile flood. Egyptians were the first civilization to switch from a lunar (moon) calendar to a solar calendar."

For some reason, every time I came to class here, I felt like the only person in the classroom and that the teacher was talking directly to me. When she spoke, I imagined ancient Egyptians gazing up to the night sky with tablets in their hands recording the stars' positions, but when she mentioned the name Sirius, the Dog Star, it got me thinking about the director and her name. But those thoughts didn't last long because Miss Guide zoomed over to another subject.

"Back to the Space Time Continuum, is it linear? Are there

other dimensions existing at the same time as we are? Or are some people born again in a time that happened already?"

After she asked this, Miss Guide walked behind her desk to look for something. My brain was stuck on what she had said about other dimensions existing at the same time. I thought about heaven, where Falafel was now—a place where he was eating rainbow ice-cream and running through fields of clouds—a place that dropped some of its essence into the ground right here at The Children's Horrible House.

While she searched, in order to not lose the class's attention, Miss Guide continued her lesson.

"Some people think Leonardo da Vinci was one of those people who was born at a time that was way behind his level of intellect. Maybe he had lived once already and brought his advanced ideas to the past making him appear way ahead of his time."

Miss Guide pulled out a big book and flipped to a page with a drawing of a strange-looking helicopter.

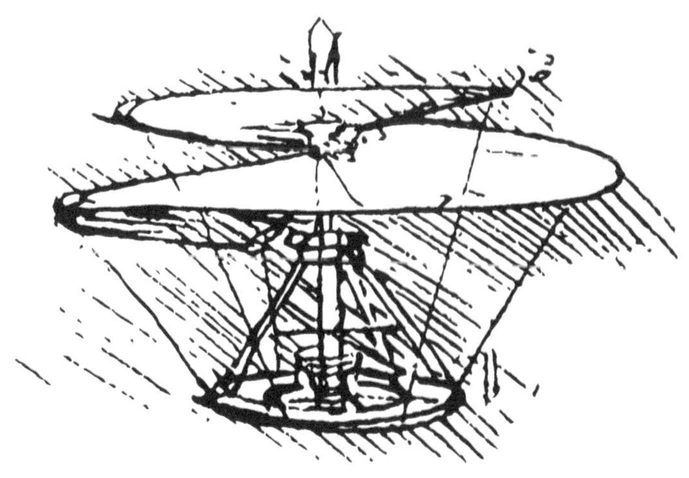

"This is da Vinci's drawing of a helicopter. Anyone want to guess when he drew this?"

I shrugged.

"This was drawn in 1493, 450 years earlier than the actual, real helicopter would be built and take flight in the air."

"Wow!" we all awed.

"This is just one example of his advanced thinking, and he's not the only person in history who seemed to have ideas way ahead of his time. Do you think these people were just gifted? Or perhaps they were lost in a place in time and space?" Miss Guide smirked after her clever rhyme.

My mind wandered through time and history. I even pondered the future. What would life be like in 200 years or in 2000 years? I had only been alive for nine years and things didn't seem much different, but when I saw old pictures of my parents when they were young or their parents, everything seemed so old and odd. The little things we took for granted, like electricity, indoor plumbing, and fast sneakers weren't around a hundred years ago. What will *they* think of next? And who were *they*? I decided to call these *theys,* "the thinkers".

CHAPTER 27
BUFFOONS

Major Whoopins and Mr. Ree lost Juniper. They couldn't find her anywhere. It was like she just slipped away in some invisible suit. After some searching and blaming one another, they decided to head back to The Children's Horrible House and hoped that no one would ask them any questions. But, of course, that was not meant to be.

"What do you mean, you lost her?" Director Pankins pounded her desk in a show of disappointment.

"She just disappeared, ma'am! I swear!" Major Whoopins said, hoping to calm her down.

"What kind of imbeciles lose a girl? She's not that small, or clever, you know!"

"Small, no … but clever, yes," Mr. Ree tried to excuse their mishap.

"Obviously cleverer than two worthless buffoons like you. Do I have to do everything around here?"

The men shared a look between them suggesting that the

director did hardly anything around here. Basically, they thought, she delegated every responsibility to everyone else.

"Miss Pankins …" Major Whoopins tried to speak.

"Out of my office!" she yelled before they could say any more. They scuttled from her office like two shamed guard dogs being dominated by a smaller female. She opened the door after they had already closed it and yelled something that was not translatable then slammed it again.

"It was your fault, man," Mr. Ree accused Major Whoopins.

"Nah … yours."

"Nope … yours."

"You couldn't wait … had to stop at Ricky T's," Major Whoopins said even though he secretly wanted to go, too.

"I was starving!"

"Shoulda waited."

"I didn't see you complaining when your mouth was stuffed with blueberry pancakes," Mr. Ree pointed out.

"Well …"

"Well …" The men continued to blame one another while they shamefully ambled along.

CHAPTER 28
The Grand Hamster

One day, Begonia was walking alone in the hallway when I saw her. She ran up to me and said, "Holly! I've been looking everywhere for you and … um …" a sheepish expression washed over her face.

"What is it?" I asked.

"I lost Dookie," she sadly reported.

"No you didn't, Begonia … I just got him from your room and brought him back to my room."

Her eyes bugged out either in relief or frustration. I signaled for her to follow me to my room and showed her Dookie who was resting in his make-shift cage on my window sill.

An unmistakable look of relief flooded her face. "I didn't lose Dookie?" Then a look of something else came over her face. "Why didn't you tell me?"

"I wanted to tell you but I guess I'm a little jealous of your friendship with Thistle and Nettle. You're always with them, and I don't like them."

"You were right, Holly. They are mean. They were just using me to make you feel bad. They didn't even like me."

I knew it! I thought, but didn't want to say *I told you so* … so I asked, "How do you know?"

"The only time they were actually nice to me was when you were around. The other times, they treated me like I had to earn their friendship and that I had to prove my loyalty to them. It got exhausting."

I knew they would turn on her and had secretly hoped they would. But I still didn't like the fact that Begonia was their victim. Even though it was different from the way they terrorized me, it was still jerky. Those girls would never learn to be nice. They were just sausage brains. At least Begonia figured this out for herself.

I reached my hand inside Dookie's cage to give him some love. When I lifted him up, there was a pile of fur balls under him. The fur balls moved! Begonia and I looked at each other with our eyes bulging. What was this?

"Dookie's a dad?" I stupidly asked.

"Ummmmm … I think Dookie is a mom!" Begonia inspected Dookie's litter. "Awe!!! They're soooooo cute! Look at them!"

Dookie was a mom? I thought Dookie was a boy this whole time.

"How did he … I mean *she* get pregnant?" I asked.

"Well, when a mommy hamster and a daddy hamster love each other very much …" she said in a silly grownup voice.

"I mean who's the daddy?" I interrupted.

"Golly, I don't know! There must be a loose boy hamster running around The Children's Horrible House! Maybe it happened when we were in the stable house?"

I looked at the babies. They were too cute! I wanted to hold them all but decided to let Dookie take care of them.

"What are you going to name them?" Begonia asked. "I think Dookie should be called something more ladylike, too … how about Cookie?"

Cookie sounded cute to me, but when I looked at my hamster, I still thought, *Dookie*. It would just have to take some time to get used to.

"What do you think we should name the babies?" I asked.

"Since there are four of them, how about Eenie, Meenie, Miney, Moe?"

"I like it! Which one is which?"

"Let's play the game to find out!"

"What game?"

"Duh, Eenie, Meenie, Miney, Moe!"

"Oh! Yeah!" We went down the line and gave each baby their new name. We then congratulated Cookie on her new babies. How exciting! I was a Grand Hamster! Or a Grandmother? No, that's not right. What was I? I wasn't sure, but I was happy … I knew that much.

CHAPTER 29
BOLDNESS AND STUPIDITY

With the new additions, Begonia's and my friendship got back on track. In fact, everyone was in sync. The only one that worried me was Juniper. No one had seen her since the day Déjeuner and the twins saw her being escorted by Major Whoopins and Mr. Ree. My suspicion was that they were bringing her back home, but I couldn't say for sure. I just had this inkling that Juniper would never leave here without me. So when I saw Mr. Ree and mean old Mr. Meanor walking down the hallway, I stopped them and asked about my sister.

"Where's Juniper?" I boldly asked.

Mr. Ree's face turned to stone while mean old Mr. Meanor's face was always stiff.

"You know what happens to squirts who think they call the shots around here?" Mr. Ree asked Mr. Meanor.

Mean old Mr. Meanor jangled his keys around indicating that if I didn't catch the hint, he'd lock me inside the hanging cage.

"That's right. So, did you want to ask another question?" Mr.

Ree asked, thinking he had taught me a lesson.

"No," I said.

He huffed, triumphantly, and said, "Thought so."

"I'll just tell you something instead." *Can you believe I said those words?* I couldn't either! What was I saying? "You better not hurt my sister in any way."

"Er what? You flippin' stinkin' meddlin' brat!'" mean old Mr. Meanor said with his face reddening and steam getting ready to puff out from his ears.

I didn't know what. I hadn't thought that far. So I said the first thing that popped into my head, "Or else". I knew that was lame, and he knew it was lame too, but it was all I could think of on such short notice. I turned slowly hoping that my dramatic gesture would save me before I slipped into Miss Leed's empty classroom. She walked in right after I did and set down a cup of tea next to a bunch of colorful crystals on her desk.

"Holly! It's not time for class yet. Did you need something?"

What I needed was a safe place to escape from Mr. Ree and mean old Mr. Meanor. But when I saw the crystals on her desk, I forgot all about those jerks. The crystals were so pretty, I wanted to touch them.

"Pretty, aren't they?" she asked, seeing my fascination with the rocks.

"Yes, they are! Where did you find them?" I asked.

She gave a little laugh, implying that it was for her to know and for me to find out before saying, "These crystals are no ordinary crystals, they come from a place so hidden, even the most decorated geologist couldn't tell you."

I had a funny feeling that she was talking about the crystal cave that Coriander and I had already explored.

"What I can tell you is that these seemingly inanimate objects are actually alive and very powerful."

"They're alive?" I asked, stunned to think that rocks were or could be alive. I imagined all the stones I had skipped into water and pictured smiley faces on them becoming scared or super excited as they bounced and whizzed into the water.

"Oh yes! Well, in a manner of speaking, of course. Crystals take time to grow just like you and I. How can you grow if you're not alive?"

She had a point.

"Did you know that there are crystals in outer space?" she asked.

"No!"

"Yes! You even have crystals growing inside of you!"

"What? Where?" I held my stomach thinking maybe eating crystals had sometimes given me bellyaches.

"In your ears!" She tugged on her own ears. I walked up to her ears and peeked inside. I didn't see any crystals poking out. I gave her a skeptical look. She was probably just joshing me. "I know you can't see them because they are so small, but there are actual salt crystals inside your ear. And if they ever go out of whack, you'll feel extremely dizzy. You might even think you're going to get sick. That's how powerful even the microscopic crystals are. Imagine even bigger ones and their potential!" she said as she picked up the largest one and held it in her palm. "I've heard that if you have the sense to hear the crystals' tones, you can transcend time."

I stared at the clear rock and became transfixed. Out of instinct, I wrapped my hands around its outer shell. It did hold a special power. Maybe it was the crystals in my ears, but I could feel the same yet weaker vibration that I had felt when I put my hands on that encrusted mirror down in the crystal cave. The gem became hot … and hotter … so hot that Miss Leeds had to set it down.

"Yeeewww! Oh my! I've never had that happen before! Dear, dear, dear!" she said hoping to calm me down. But I was already calm. I wanted to tell her that that wasn't the first time that it had happened to me. Instead I stayed quiet. "Are you okay, Holly?"

"Yes, I'm okay. I guess I just didn't expect that to happen."

"I didn't either!"

"But you said," I started then cut myself off. I didn't want to make Miss Leeds feel bad.

"Oh, I know what I said. It's just that sometimes you're told things and then you tell others about what you've been told, but when you actually experience something, that's a whole other thing." She gave me a quirky smile. "I'm sorry … did any of that make any sense?"

"Believe it or not, it made perfect sense." I smiled, too.

Her next class was slowly filing in so I started to make my exit so she could prepare.

"Hey, Holly," Miss Leeds called out.

"Yes?" I turned around.

"That was pretty cool though, wasn't it?"

"Yeah, it was …" I said before I stepped into the hallway where Coriander was waiting for me.

"What was pretty cool?" he asked.

"Oh! You have no idea!"

"I know; that's why I'm asking, duh."

"You have crystals in your ears," I blurted.

"Oh … kay …" he said with his left eyebrow lower than the other.

"I'm serious!"

"No, you're Holly," he said in a jokingly serious way.

It was my turn to tilt my head. "Never mind, I guess you just had to be there."

"Did you hear that there was going to be a talent show on Star Day?"

That was a quick change of subject, I thought, but I was glad of it. "Yes, I did hear about that, everyone has. Do you have a special talent that you never told me about?"

"Yes, it's called when everyone is preoccupied with the show, that's when we will have enough time to find the treasure."

"I never heard of that talent before!" I sarcastically said.

"Well, I happen to be the best at it. Want to join me?"

"But of course!" I said. Then we laid out our plans for finding the house's hidden treasure.

After we discussed every detail, we were quietly imagining the events. Coriander snuck a sly smile and said, "Told you that you'd care about the 'stupid' treasure again." I rolled my eyes knowing he was right.

CHAPTER 30
SPUNKY SNEAKERS

Outside the window, a cheerful morning was rising. It just happened to be our free day where we could do whatever we wanted. I needed to be outdoors to get some fresh air. After I made my bed and ate breakfast, I skipped outside.

The breeze was soft and the sky was clear with the exception of a few stubborn clouds. I noticed that the moon was still out even though it was obviously daytime. What was the moon still doing out here? Didn't it know it was the sun's turn to shine? It continued to shine even with my silent scolding.

Déjeuner, Clover, and Begonia were playing with Cookie and her babies. Begonia and I shared hamster duties. I loved how everyone loved my hamsters. Begonia was a natural when it came to animal care. I trusted her completely. I walked over, sat with my legs crossed among my circle of friends, and thought about how lucky I was to have such excellent buddies. The only missing playmate was Juniper. Where was she? It was just like when I was home. I was always wondering where she was. In my heart, I knew she was okay. Juniper was special that way. Even if we weren't together, I could feel her and sense that she was thinking about me.

I got distracted when I saw some of the other kids racing each other. It was fun watching them compete. I naturally wanted in on the action so I put myself in the running.

First match was against a heavier boy who had just beaten a skinnier girl. I whooped him. It was no contest. I ran like a gazelle thanks to my super-fast sneakers. These Pro-Wingers still had lots of spunk in their worn treads. Next match was against a tall lanky girl who looked imposing at first. She went down like the first guy. Even though she was tall, she was slow … super slow. I almost felt bad for beating her so badly.

Next, I matched up with a girl who had twists of hair in three sections around her head held by cherry-tipped hair bands.

"On your mark, get set, go!" the heavier boy called.

I took off like usual; only this time, my opponent stayed beside me. I ran harder. She ran harder and faster until I was clearly behind her. I looked down at my sneakers which were starting to smoke with extra effort. They just didn't have any more to give or maybe that was my legs and lungs. She whooped me and my racing days were over.

Boy, was I out of breath. I looked around for my girlfriends but I guess they scrammed while I was racing. Maybe they didn't want to see me lose. Or maybe they didn't want to let me see that I saw them see me lose? Or whatever … I lost.

But someone did see me lose and stuck around to laugh at my defeat … Coriander.

"Did you really think you had a chance? Look at her! She was born to run," Coriander stated the obvious. Her long muscular limbs made my wet noodle legs look silly.

"I see that now, but …" I said, still out of breath. We walked around the grounds of The Children's Horrible House not wanting to stay while the victor celebrated. Even though she clearly deserved to gloat, it wounded my sneakers' ego … or maybe it was my ego that was hurt.

I had no desire to go indoors. We were always inside, so when we were allowed outside or we snuck outside, I wanted to linger as long as possible. The sun warmed my skin as I faced it like a flower. I closed my eyes and stared at the back of my eyelids. I could see the sun's shape through them which looked like an orange glowing ball. My eyes crossed behind my lids; I opened them when I felt a little dizzy.

"C'mon." Coriander nudged me from my momentary sun gazing before we meandered around the grounds.

We walked to the tree that I had fallen from the last time we were here. I looked up the trunk wondering how I could have been so clumsy. It looked like such a perfect climbing tree that I felt the need to climb it again.

"Race you to the top!" I challenged.

"Oh, you are on!" Coriander pushed me out of the way.

"Hey! That's not fair!"

"That's what losers always say!" he taunted.

That was enough to ignite a fire in me to climb faster than ever. I kept tugging at his pants to gain on him, then he'd find a way around me until we found ourselves at the tip and weakest part of the tree.

It swayed entirely too much with the steady breeze.

"Whoa! I'm scared, Coriander."

"You would be," he teased. "Go ahead, admit your defeat, and then I'll let you climb back down."

The breeze picked up and tossed me around.

"You won," I quickly admitted.

"Well, I'm glad we agree," he smiled as I scurried back down to the stronger branches. He followed me down. We sat together safely on a thick sturdy limb.

After our skirmish, we sat observing the growing garden from this vantage. It was ridiculously amazing. It looked like a fluorescent-hued hurricane or spiral galaxy spinning in slow motion. The tomb of Hawthorne North Star could barely be detected. All we could see was the tip of the dome because the garden was growing around it.

My thoughts began to drift with the gentle breezes. The air was fresh and warm, like a laundered blanket. It covered me in comfort. I thought about the last time I was in this tree, how I had seen the glowing garden for the first time, and subsequently, the mausoleum. I thought about how close we were to finding out the secret this house and estate wanted to tell. I looked over at the looming mansion and felt bad for its limitations on speech. It had a story, and it was doing everything in its power to set itself free, but no one spoke its language, maybe … until now.

"What if it's not a real treasure?" I asked Coriander out of the blue. "What if the prize is only valuable for the Star family and has nothing to do with us?"

"Do you really think Sirius Pankins would choose to stay here just for some family token? No, I know her better than that."

"How?"

"How what?"

"How do you know her better?"

"Do you think you have to be friends with someone to know them?" he asked.

I couldn't figure out what he was trying to tell me. Thankfully, he made himself more clear. "I mean you are definitely not friends with Thistle and Nettle but you know their nature, right? You know they are up to no good, no matter what they are doing, right?"

I knew with certainty those girls were jerks. I did not need to be friends with them to know this. "I guess I can see what you're saying."

"I've been watching them, and I know that they are up to something big, and it's about to happen."

I nodded my head in agreement but then rethought his sentence. Why would he be watching those dimwits? "Thistle and Nettle?"

"No! Not them … they're just … you know," he said.

"Who is them, then?"

"Miss Pankins, Miss Judge, and that old guy."

"Who is the old guy?"

"Reed Trustworthy."

Reed Trustworthy, I had heard that name before. I sorted through all the names I had heard from here and found a potential match. "Do you mean Hawthorne Star's old butler?"

"Yes."

At that moment, a bug flew into my open mouth just as I inhaled. It got close to my down shoot and my throat closed before I coughed it back up. Coriander banged my back. I spit out the little buggy and shook off a chill of disgust.

"I thought he had died," I said while Coriander gave me a look of concern.

"Apparently not." Coriander sounded so much more sophisticated when he talked about this kind of stuff—like his soul was older. I looked at him as he continued to speak and saw something

I had never noticed before. He was handsome, for a boy. His sandy blonde hair ruffled in the breeze and when he set his glass-green eyes on me, I could see what Begonia saw in him. He looked like he was from a former time. A time when boys grew more mature than they do nowadays. I had never looked at him like that before. He was just my friend, but upon closer inspection, he had me guessing. Maybe *he was* from another time, like Leonardo da Vinci?

"I've been reading about something with Miss Judge in the library."

"With Miss Judge?" I asked thinking that Coriander would never talk to her again after she had surprised us with her true identity. "But I thought ..."

"I still do, but I'm telling you, she is the one who you have to watch out for. Have you ever heard, 'Keep your friends close and your enemies closer'?"

"No," I said.

"Now you have. Anyway, you and I need to go talk to her together because what she thinks is possible, is pretty unbelievable."

"Why can't you just tell me now?"

"Because."

"Because, why?"

"Geez, sometimes you are so immature, Holly."

"Uh uh!"

"Uh huh!"

CHAPTER 31
SNEAKY SLIPPING SOUNDS

My stomach had been bothering me ever since breakfast. It felt cramped and tight so when I lay down to go to sleep, I could hear my guts gurgling while they wandered within my belly. I tried to get my mind off of the discomfort by watching Cookie and her babies all huddled together for their evening slumber. Cookie was a good mommy by making sure her pups were thoroughly bathed and fed.

My stomach grumbled. Suddenly I could feel a bubble in it. When I turned to my side, I felt something weird so I pushed on my belly and a fart slipped out a lot louder than I would have preferred. It sounded like a jet ski sputtering with a big blast at the end to cap it off.

PFT putt putt Pft putt PFFFFFtttt PLFFFT!!!!

Déjeuner sat up like a Halloween decoration popping out of a coffin and asked, "Holly? Was that you?"

Rightfully embarrassed, I thought about my mom and her belly aches. I guess our gas was genetic … I had the same stomach-achy farts as my mom.

Phooey.

Now, how could I pretend that wasn't *my* fart? I swished my blankets around trying to make my bed squeak but nothing captured the sound of my genuine fart. Other girls giggled and slowly sat up wondering if I would take credit for my cheek squeek.

"It was Holly; she farted!" Camellia announced while my face flooded red. But since the lights were turned off, no one could see my blush.

"Okay, yes. I farted. Geez what's the big deal?" I confessed.

All the girls started laughing which, of course, made it so I couldn't help but giggle, too. I mean, what are you going to do? When you have to fart, you have to fart! And when you fart, you have to laugh … plain and simple. As the whooping wound down another blast erupted from someone else's butt. I immediately announced that it was not me!

"It was me!" Déjeuner said in her mouse-like voice.

"Oh my gosh! You guys are fart machines!" Camellia declared as the light turned on, and Miss Place stormed into the room.

"All right! Now that's enough! You are going to earn yourselves an extra hour of bed-making if you keep up these shenanigans."

Everyone zipped their lips and became still. No one wanted to make any more beds than we already had to. All the girls settled down as Miss Place left the room. Quiet calmness entered the room as everyone began to relax until a long flatus fizzer invaded our ears. But this time, we all shook in our sheets, laughing as quietly as possible so we wouldn't get in trouble, but it was too late. Miss Place came back in and said, "You got it, one more hour … want to make it two?" No one else farted or moved a muscle until morning.

And by morning, I mean extra early morning. Miss Place woke

us up an hour earlier so that we could fit in our punishment. I have *NEVER* loved waking up early in the morning … actually, I had one exception … Christmas morning. On Christmas, I couldn't wake up early enough. I remember one time I had snuck downstairs, tiptoed to the living room, and saw the Christmas tree sparkle with lights, ornaments, and tinsel. Surrounding the tree was a mountain of gifts; I scanned the gifts in order to find the ones for me.

One extra-special Christmas, I got my red BMX bike, which I loved more than any other gift. I knew I was going to break records with the speedy two-wheeler. I rode it around and around my driveway, did bunny hops, and wheelies too! The only thing that got me off that bike was Christmas dinner. My mom made the best turkey, ham, potatoes, carrots, and casseroles.

That year we had The Cornpickle Family from church come over to share in our celebration. Mrs. Cornpickle had extra-big nostrils especially when she sang. The night before, on Christmas Eve, we had all gone to church and Mrs. Cornpickle sang in the Christmas Cantata. She sang one of my favorites called "Oh Night Divine" or at least that's what I called it. I'll never forget the way she performed …

Fall on your knees,
Oh hear the angel's voices
Oh, ni—ght divine!

When the notes soared higher, her nostrils flared wider, rounder, and deeper, which made us naughty kids giggle. On the way home, riding in one of my father's old jalopies, we used our index fingers and thumbs to make circles, held them up to our noses, replicating the shapes that Mrs. Cornpickle's nostrils made on their own. They were quite impressive … and funny.

What wasn't funny, was our morning's punishment. I had zero incentive to want to wake up. There were no presents for me to open, no stockings to empty, no Christmas music, or special dinner, just beds that needed making, sad songs, and gross food—not motivational at all.

But we worked until we were freed for breakfast. While I was walking in to the dining hall, Coriander was rushing out.

What's the hurry? Where was he heading? I had to find out, no matter how hungry I was.

CHAPTER 32
HAUNTING GROUNDS

The aging man found himself lingering in different areas around the house while everyone else slept. This night, he went to an old familiar domicile and found the room's air to be heavy with regret. During his tenure, Reed had spent more time in Hawthorne North Star's chamber than in his own smaller, humbler room. These walls had witnessed many conversations between he and his employer. They knew Reed well.

Next to the oversized chair, he lit the lamp and casually scooped up the old broken Indian doll that Saffron used to play with. He sat there softly caressing the hair and cheeks. This doll represented something much bigger than anyone knew. Sings-in-the-Meadow had this doll made for her daughter while she was pregnant. Reed was in love with Sings-in-the-Meadow, but so was Hawthorne.

Reed knew his own feelings were forbidden. He felt inadequate and had no wealth nor name to offer her. Little did he know, that his brave love would have been plenty. It pained him beyond measure to see her go. He tried everything he could to keep her. Even a life of luxury that she would find in a marriage to Hawthorne North Star couldn't satisfy her. At the time, neither man knew that possessions, wealth, and power had zero influence on Sings-in-the-Meadow.

Her treasures were true love, honesty, and respecting the magic in nature. Those things were passed down through generations in her bloodline. It was not something that could be concocted. In order to keep the balance that she had so earnestly tried to maintain, she felt that her presence in this house and the potential heartbreak she would cause, made it so her only option was to leave. But she could not steal the child. That would have been selfish on her part. Their love birthed a child who was a treasure. Sings-in-the-Meadow gave Saffron, as a parting gift to her father.

Reed held the doll, wishing he could ask the universe to send Sings-in-the Meadow back to him. Why had he thought her beliefs were so far-fetched? It wasn't until she was gone that what she had tried to teach him before made sense. Her lessons reverberated through time and spoke when truth could be manifested. When he understood them, he used them to influence the children who came to stay at The Hawthorne House for Children. The results spoke for themselves. He was happy to find that Saffron, a.k.a Sirius Pankins, had at least continued the lessons he and Hawthorne had implemented. But they only knew so much. If he could just go back in time, he would give anything for a moment to just listen to Sings-in-the-Meadow. Her voice was smooth, calm, nearly angelic, and filled with wisdom emanating from her ancient roots.

It seemed that the universe heard his request. As he held the head of the doll, by happenstance, he looked inside the neck and found a rolled up piece of paper. He pulled it out, unrolling it. It was a note written in Sings-in-the-Meadow's native language. It was meant for Saffron, her daughter. He knew little about the language, so he took the doll and scroll to the library where he could translate the letter more accurately.

After cross-referencing each symbol to its English counterpart, he was stunned to read aloud the contents of the note.

"Dear Saffron, my Radiant Star," he said and then the words became too controversial to read out loud. After he finished, he reread it to make sure he had actually understood the words correctly. He still couldn't believe it.

In a flash, his whole life was turned upside down. Everything that he once believed about himself, Saffron, and Sings-in-the-Meadow was horribly wrong. But what could he do? What would he do?

CHAPTER 33

WHEN DREAMS DANCE WITH NIGHTMARES

Sirius tossed around in her bed like a puppet lead by scenes being played out before her subconscious mind. She was walking in the glowing garden as a sparkly light seeped into the ground then became smothered by dirt. The ground became so soft that she began to sink. She twisted and turned, but the quicksand swallowed her whole. She couldn't breathe because she was afraid she would inhale dirt and suffocate. Then the bottom fell out from underneath her, and she was in a cave that radiated just like the glowing garden. Looking around she saw her once hidden treasure. It was filled with everything a treasure hunter would want: golden jeweled crowns, dripping diamond pendants, and pearls strung like garland. Candlesticks, chalices, and ornate furniture covered in gold and silver took up one side of the cave. She wanted to cover herself in the treasure, but before she did, a soft voice spoke from the other side of the room. She looked but couldn't see anyone.

"Saffron! Saffron! Come to me!"

She looked twice at her treasure before following the voice. She couldn't find anyone. The treasure started to melt into a green goo that hissed. It had turned into snakes. Their hisses became more violent as they reached out to strike her. She jumped back as her feet began to sink into the oozing gunk.

The voice called again, "Saffron! Saffron! Come to me!"

Upon turning around, a mirror with a burst of light projecting from it spoke, "Come to …" the voice got deeper and slower. "Come …" deeper still. When she tried to get to it, everything vanished, including her … until she woke up sweating. This wasn't the first time she had a bad dream, but she hoped it would be the last. She couldn't help but wonder what it could possibly mean.

CHAPTER 34
The Solar Cross

It took another week before we were able to talk to Miss Judge, but it was worth the wait. Coriander and I spent our whole free day, which seemed to pass too quickly, if you can believe that, in the library. But since it was grey and stormy out, there was little else to do.

I walked over to the wall of windows to watch as clouds jostled with one another, bumping, and becoming bigger with each movement. I wondered if they ever got mad at each other or if they just got on with their business of rainmaking. The garden was soaking up all this wetness, growing at a ludicrous speed, taking over the whole estate while looking more and more monstrous in its movements. I became concerned when I felt something gently slither around my legs. I jumped.

"What in the world?" I looked down while a beautiful Siamese kitty stared at me waiting for attention. *He looked familiar*, I thought.

This must be the kitty I saw that night in Hawthorne North Star's chamber. After regaining my composure, I gladly gave him a rub.

"Holly, over here," Coriander loudly whispered.

I turned as he and Miss Judge were surrounding a table with a stack of big fat books. I looked back at the kitty, who had found other bookshelves to mark with his scent, before scuffing over to their work station.

"How have you been, Holly?" Miss Judge asked in her usual disarming tone. What was it about her that made me like her when I saw her but had second thoughts about her when I wasn't around her?

"I'm good." I looked at Coriander who was giving me a weird look.

"What?" I asked him.

"Nothing," he waved off my question.

Miss Judge cleared her throat. Coriander looked down, not wanting to make eye contact. I fidgeted with my fingernails. This was more uncomfortable than I had imagined.

"I'm sorry," Miss Judge said.

We both looked up at her, but she looked directly at me.

"For?" I asked because I wondered why she was apologizing to me, but I guess it sounded the same way parents ask children to explain why they are sorry.

She cleared her throat again and thought briefly before answering me.

"For not being forthright," she said.

"About what?" I asked still sounding like a parent but really wanting to know her response.

"About my true identity."

"Oh, that's okay," I said forgiving her.

"Really?"

"Yeah, I understand why you had to be sneaky; you were just trying to figure out who your family was. It's understandable."

"Oh, yes … thank you for forgiving me, Holly."

"You're welcome," I said as I pulled out a heavy chair ready to get down to business.

"Miss Judge and I have been on a secret mission, and if what we have discovered is true, we are on the cusp of something unbelievable," Coriander said in a tone he used when he was super excited.

"What is it?" I asked.

"Do you remember how last year's Star Day was celebrated at the height of The Star of Panivita's conjunction period?" he asked.

I thought about how the planets Jupiter, Venus, and the star Regulus came into alignment to form the bright Star of Panivita and pictured the magnificent sight. A puzzle in outer space came together for us to see.

"Yes."

"Well, this year's Star Day is going to be even more … um … crazy."

"Crazy?" I thought he was going to say more spectacular, not crazy. "How so?"

Miss Judge flipped through one of her books and stopped on a page with a bunch of planets and stars with white lines connecting them. While looking at the pictures of outer space, I couldn't help but marvel at the cosmos' grandness. It's like this whole other world surrounding our world. After flipping through some of the pages, I found the size difference between Earth and Jupiter—Earth is tiny by comparison. But Jupiter is puny in relation to our Sun, which happens to be a star. I was stunned to find that our Sun is microscopic in contrast to Sirius, the Dog Star, and that's not the biggest star out there! Miss Judge let me wander through the pages before she flipped back to the subject at hand.

Awe inducing words eagerly popped out from the pages like they were spring-loaded with information I could not ignore. I'll just read them to you because they were too important to misread. I read, "The derivation of the name Sirius is from the ancient Greek word for *glowing* or *scorched*." The speech that the director had given at the assembly replayed in my mind ... *Many years ago I drew up plans for a garden*. So maybe that's why the garden Sirius Pankins planned glowed—the glowing garden was named that because of her! But then I thought about the other meaning, scorched. Those were two very different meanings. One meant something brilliant, luminous, and bright while the other meant devastation, destruction, and its aftermath—both translations had occurred to Sirius Pankins' garden.

I guess you *could* speak things into existence even just by a name. A feeling of awe, suspicion, and wonderment came over me as I relished discovering something of this magnitude.

"This year's Star Day is unlike any other year, unless you go back fifty years ago. As you can see here ..." Miss Judge pointed to a picture of a bright star with a cross around it, like the solar cross. "These are two stars, actually. Sirius A, the big one you see here is the brightest star in our nighttime sky, along with its much smaller faint stellar companion, Sirius B. In this picture, you can see that astronomers overexposed the image of Sirius A so that the dimmer Sirius B could be seen. The cross-shaped diffraction spikes and concentric rings around Sirius A, and the small ring around Sirius

B, are artifacts produced within the telescope's imaging system. The two stars revolve around each other every fifty years forming a solar cross," Miss Judge said breaking up my new found abstraction.

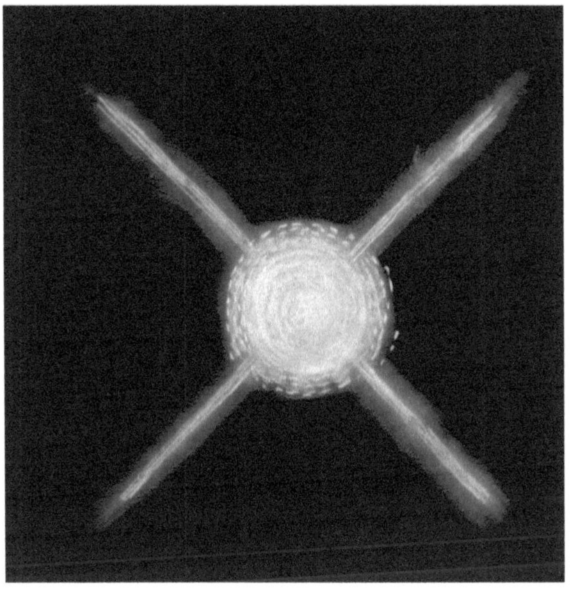

"Like the symbol around this whole estate?" I asked but also wondered if all this was coincidental. "So the solar cross isn't around our sun?"

"This one is around Sirius which is a star, and our Sun is a star as well—just not nearly as big as Sirius. But on the same day, which is why I said this Star Day is truly unique, there will be a solar eclipse. These rare phenomena, where the moon casts a shadow blocking out the sun's rays, are in themselves quite substantial. But for these events to occur at the same time, is possibly a miracle."

"I wonder if any of this has to do with the director—her name and its meaning and the fact that it is coming up so soon," I said.

"The probability of all this being random and occurring conjunctively is astronomical in itself," Coriander spoke as if he had turned into some sort of rocket scientist.

Miss Judge chimed in saying, "A little known fact is that this estate used to be home to the Blackfeet Indians. Long before anything was ever built here, the tribe would move with the seasons and the bison. This was their territory. When they were driven from this area, their mystical influence stayed behind within the land."

I thought about the glowing garden and how it illuminated with each step, how the magically lit orbs floated around like dreams, and the moonflowers that unfurled as darkness took over. This place was truly mystical for sure. The native tribes must have been in tune with its magic.

"When my father purchased this land, he knew it was special, but it wasn't until he met Sings-in-the-Meadow that he learned just how exceptional it was."

"Who put all the symbols around here?" I asked.

"My father did, apparently because he found the markings in the trees and other various brandings around the estate. He must have decided that the symbol was this land's identity, not knowing what it really meant until …"

"Sings-in-the-Meadow?"

"Correct."

"What does this have to do with his birthday?"

"That just happens to be coincidental … no, I take that back. Nothing is coincidental. Sometimes we don't know the reason for a link at first, so *that*, my dear, will come in time … like everything else it seems." She patted me on the shoulder, reassuring me of her promise. "But back to your question about his birthday, it just so happens to occur at the height of the solar cross, and with this being a geological hotspot, we are in for quite a show. I just don't know what to expect or if I'm right." Before Miss Judge finished speaking, the cat jumped up on the table and decided to lie on top of the books after getting some attention from Coriander and me.

"Oh Copper! He just loves attention," Miss Judge scolded the kitty, but the cat's eyes tuned her out as they regally blinked.

"Geological hotspot? What does that mean?" I got back to the point.

"Have you noticed the strange phenomena occurring here? The glowing garden, lightening directly striking it, the star shower, and now our horrible galactic growing garden? Do you think it's all just coincidence?"

"Maybe it's because of the crystal cave under the ground? Miss Leeds told me about the power of crystals, small and large. Even the tiny crystals in our ears can cause a whole body to go off balance. Imagine what a whole cave filled with gigantic crystals is capable of!"

Coriander cleared his throat as if I should shut my mouth.

"So, you've been to the crystal cave, I take it," Miss Judge said.

I looked over at Coriander and decided it was too late to put those words back in my mouth so I waited for him to speak. Evidently, I had said too much.

"Yes, we found it when we were being held in the stable house," he offered.

"Aha!" she said as if she had suspected our visit. "It's spectacular, isn't it?"

We sheepishly agreed. Everyone got quiet for a second while we tried to gauge the depth of where this conversation would go. After enough discomfort, Miss Judge asked, "Did you happen to notice that mirror?"

"YES!" I said. "It almost burned me!" Evidently I spoke with too much excitement because Copper sprang up and ran away.

"Well, there you go, that's the answer to your question."

I scratched my head, "What question?"

"The geological hotspot … there's your spot," Miss Judge said casually.

Mind blown …

CHAPTER 35
KABOOM

My mind was blown. I looked over at Coriander who also had a strange look on his face. I couldn't tell if it was good or bad.

"Basically, this land, and in particular the mirror in the crystal cave, is a geological hotspot not just for the ancient peoples who knew its power but for the universe itself."

I felt unworthy of this information. This was too big, too important, too miraculous! "Why are you sharing all this with me?"

Miss Judge stood in front of me, looked deeply into my eyes, and lifted my chin. "Because you're special, remember?"

I thought maybe Miss Judge was messing with me. But then I remembered the last time I was here, how I had convinced her of my special powers when I was always able to find the book, *Sage Themes,* that she had not been able to locate on her own. I wondered, what about me was so lucky? *Maybe* just by saying that I was "special", made me "*special*".

"Oh, yeah! I am special," I said with a wink.

Coriander just shook his head, like I was some sort of crazy coot.

I had a strange thought. It came out of nowhere and I blurted out, "It's in the books!"

"What?" Miss Judge asked.

"Where are they? Where are *Sage Themes* and *The Message*?" I questioned.

"They're in Director Pankins' office," Miss Judge said.

"We need to get them as soon as possible," I said with more urgency than necessary.

CHAPTER 36
THE GETAWAY AND THE GET BACK

Juniper had a feeling that those two knuckleheads would let down their guard around food time. She had waited until they were fully engrossed in their pancakes before making her getaway. She had pretended to use the restroom but instead used the restaurant's phone to call Hyperion who was glad to come pick her up. He was not as excited when she had told him to bring her right back to where he had last left her.

"This place gives me the heebie-jeebies, Juniper. Just let me take you back home for Peter's sake!"

"Peter's sake? I thought it was Pete's sake."

"Pete … Peter, Paul, and Mary … you know what I mean."

"I will definitely let you take me home when I get Holly back," Juniper said in a sweet coaxing fashion.

"Holly's here at your grandparents, now?"

"Um … yes … she is … here … at my grandparents." Juniper nodded while trying to sound convincing.

"Wait, I'm confused, why were you …?"

Juniper cut him off saying, "Hyperion, I don't have time for all these questions right this instant, but when you come back to get me, I will tell you *everything*."

Hyperion twisted his mouth around trying to read what *everything* meant but knew Juniper too well to prod her when her mind was made up.

"Thanks again, Doodle Muffin," Juniper said in one of her childish voices and gave him a peck before getting out of the car.

She ran toward the fiery gate, squeezed through an opening, and was met with the glaring gigantic mansion. She heard some whistling and keys jangling before seeing Mr. Meanor rounding a corner. Quickly, she ducked behind some bushes until he passed. After the coast was clear, she tried to figure out the best way inside the house.

"I knew you'd be back!"

Juniper jumped when she heard the voice exclaim from behind her.

"Cheese and rice!!! Oh my heavens, you scared me!" Juniper said as she held her pounding heart.

Déjeuner ran up to hug her. Clover came up too and said, "There you are! And there you are, too! Junipah, where have you been? We've been lookin' all ovah for you!"

Juniper reached out and hugged both girls. They each took turns embracing, genuinely happy to see one another.

"Where did they take you?" Clover asked.

Juniper snickered a little when she said, "Ricky T's Pancake Piles."

"Huh?" Clover and Déjeuner said in unison. "They took you to get pancakes?"

"Not exactly, but that's where I escaped. Director Pankins tried to send me home, but I won't be going anywhere without Holly."

"Oh yeah."

"And you guys either! I couldn't just leave you here all alone!" Juniper said in one of her gremlin-sounding voices.

Their faces brightened.

"Do you think Director Pankins will let you stay here if she finds you?"

"To be on the safe side, I'm going to hide in the stable house."

"That's too scary! You can't be there all alone! No, I won't let you be there all alone!" Déjeuner pleaded.

"I don't have many other options," Juniper said.

"We'll think of somethin'," Clover insisted.

CHAPTER 37
The Message

"We'll have to sneak into her office when we know she won't be there." Coriander said.

"Yes, that's a good idea!" I agreed.

Coriander rolled his eyes because obviously he knew his idea was good.

"When is the best time for us to sneak in?" he asked Miss Judge.

"That's going to be tricky. She doesn't exactly have a schedule; believe me, I know."

"We just need to get the books and bring them here. Then we can bring them back before she notices that they're missing," I said trying to form a plan.

"We need the mirror that is in her office though," Miss Judge informed us.

"Why?"

"When we held the books up to the mirror, you could see big letters shaped like roots that spelled out a short poem. Hold on, let me go get it so I don't forget something."

Miss Judge went down one of the aisles then we heard a door open and shut. After about five minutes, she came back with a journal. She opened it, flipped to the right page, and read aloud:

At the height of the Dog Star's bright blue cross,
One to reunite with love that's lost.
Every once in a wrinkle or fifty even years,
Earth opens up to release hardened tears.
A universe found through gates of living stone;
clear and powerful to break the bone.
From The Meadow where time stands still,
lies the other side … if you see, you will.

"Can I see it?" I asked. Hearing a poem was nice, but I needed to look at the words to read them for myself. "This was written in *Sage Themes*?"

"No, this one was in *The Message.* There was no poem in *Sage Themes,*" Miss Judge said.

"Are you sure? Why would only one of the books have this message?" Coriander asked.

"I think you just answered your own question," Miss Judge explained.

"Oh, because of its message … the poem was *The Message* … I get it," I said thinking that I had *gotten* it.

"So what's the point about the other book, *Sage Themes*?" Coriander asked.

"It has another message and it isn't through a mirror," I said as my eyes became glossy and trance-like. I began to visualize what I had seen when Director Pankins and Miss Judge had me looking at the book. I hadn't seen anything until I took off my glasses. And then I saw everything in the book moving and popping out like holograms.

"How do you know?" Coriander doubted.

"Because I saw it with my eyes … my 80-year-old-granny eyes."

"What do you mean?" he asked.

"Get me the book, and I'll tell you exactly what I mean."

* * *

"I'll be right back," Miss Judge said as she was already walking out of the library.

Coriander and I sat quietly for some time while waiting for Miss Judge to return. Eventually I stood and walked around looking up to the sky-blue painted ceilings filled with swirling clouds. Through the aisles of books, I came to a wall that seemed to be over thirty feet tall stuffed with books from floor to ceiling. I stepped onto the bottom rung of a ladder on wheels that made every book accessible. With a few little kicks, I took a ride back and forth along the wall. I started having a little too much fun when Coriander stopped my jaunt.

"Hey!" I cried out. "Why'd you do that?"

"Miss Judge is back with Director Pankins."

"Phooey! Why is she here?" I asked.

"Because she has something that she wants to know!" Director Pankins said a little too loudly. There was no trace of a smile on her face, only determination turning to desperation. She looked less put together than normal. Her dark hair hung loose over her shoulders. Her usual black skirt was replaced with a nightgown, slippers, and a grey robe. She was rubbing her eyes. What was going on with her?

"Oh, yes ma'am," I obediently stepped off the ladder and followed them back to the table. Miss Judge had an impatient look on her face, and I wasn't sure if it was directed toward me or the director.

"Now, Holly, is it?" Miss Pankins asked, knowing very well who I was, "Tell me what you see." She signaled for Coriander to pull out the chair for me to sit.

I instantly felt cold and insecure as a shiver ran down my spine. Maybe it was Miss Pankins frosty breath that fell from her mouth as she hunched over me.

I opened the book, turned to a page filled with drawings, diagrams, and captions. It looked ordinary as usual. I took off my glasses; then it all popped out from the page just like it had before. I saw planets in outer space moving, and forming a solar system. In a different constellation, another system formed but with a much larger, brighter sun. A beam of light flashed from the center of the sun which shined into a mirror that shattered. A raging storm-like entity came into view destroying everything in its path. Buildings were blown to bits. The leftover debris flew into the air then turned into a swirling kaleidoscope of beautiful blue butterflies. The devastation was transformed into a calm meadow filled with bison, flowers, and long grass that swayed in the breeze.

"I can't take this anymore. For crying out loud! Tell me!! What do you see?" Director Pankins demanded.

"Ask nicer!" Miss Judge said.

"I'll be nicer when she tells me what I want to hear!" she roared.

"I don't think you want to hear what I saw, Miss Pankins," I said.

"I don't care what you think I want to hear. I want to hear what you saw, nothing about what you think."

"If you weren't so cruel or mean when you spoke, she would have told you already," Miss Judge argued. The ladies went back and forth until I cut in with a low voice saying, "I saw you and everything in this house get destroyed. Are you happy now?"

The director blinked as did Miss Judge. Coriander's face flinched slightly.

"She's lying," Miss Pankins said, then looked directly at me, "and for that, you'll be locked up in THE DUNGEON until you tell me the truth."

"It is the truth! I saw it! A beam of light blows up the mirror, then a black shadow takes everything and nothing is left but a meadow filled with bison."

Everyone was quiet as my words sank into their skulls. Coriander scanned my face to see if what I said was true. I returned his glare with a look that said, *of course it's true.*

Copper jumped on to the table with a funny little meow scaring everyone from their silence. "Oh, you silly kitty! What am I going to do with you?" Miss Judge said as she wrapped her arms around him. I was grateful for his intrusion. I turned around to see if Director Pankins was still behind me but she wasn't. I heard the library doors close but never saw her go. What was she up to?

CHAPTER 38
THE QUIET HOUR

Reed sat drinking his coffee early in the morning's mist. He liked his mornings alone, in his not so secret hideaway. He was attempting to clear his mind, but pesky thoughts kept invading his calm. Steam rose from his cup fogging his vision. As he blew on the hot drink, he blinked. When his eyes opened, he watched a girl walking from the stable house toward the main house. She wasn't little like most of the children here. He figured out who she was and wondered what she was doing out there until he saw two younger girls meeting her with a basket before they all turned back toward the stable house. A little bit later, another girl was running over there. What was going on? He stood to go investigate when the director walked up as if nothing was out of the ordinary. What *was* out of ordinary was the director. She looked unwell. He didn't want to alarm her so he stayed quiet about what he'd witnessed.

"I haven't slept in days," she announced. He looked at her bloodshot eyes and disheveled hair.

"Are you okay?" he asked.

"I feel like I'm about to lose everything."

Reed pondered her statement. "Did you ever really have anything? Do any of us?"

"Let's not get philosophical, please."

"Okay, then what do you feel you are about to lose?"

"My life," she said forlornly.

"Well, I suppose you're right … that is everything."

She hunched in a way he had never seen her stand. He thought she was just being overly dramatic as she had a tendency to be but something told him otherwise.

"It's just this feeling I have. Plus, I keep having this nightmarish dream that in order for me to get what I want most in the world, I would have to die."

"What is it that you want most in the world?" he asked.

Sirius knew what she wanted, and it made her feel awkward to know its truth. She wanted it so badly that she felt foolish to wish for it—because she was sure it would never happen. It was too big, too ambitious, and she knew it. But she couldn't stop herself from wanting something always beyond her grasp. Tears filled her eyes and plopped onto the courtyard stone.

Her head was turned down as her shoulders slumped. Out of nowhere, the child, Saffron, that Reed loved, appeared. His heart melted. He stood up, grabbed her to him, and hugged her. For the first time in decades, Director Pankins was embraced by someone who truly loved her. She didn't pull away, but she didn't know how to respond so she simply let him soothe her. His deep voice echoed from his chest in short empathetic hums. He didn't say a word, just communicated through his gestures and *they* said so much more. By her not pulling away, she said enough, too.

After some time, they sat together in contemplative silence. They offered one another grace, peace, and comfort, which they both needed so desperately. After being self-reliant and independent for so long, they had become used to the rigid, cold, lifeless existence they had both endured. Yet they held on to hope for something wildly different. What lay on the horizon of their destinies would not only take them by surprise, it would rewrite the definitions of their whole lives. Nothing and no one could have prepared them for its impending arrival.

CHAPTER 39
SQUARE DANCING

Déjeuner held onto Begonia's arm as she was led to the stable house to bring Juniper her food. I was walking just behind them with a jug of juice.

When they told me that Juniper was back, I couldn't wait to see her. The girls carried a basket overflowing with mediocre food. Juniper was foraging through it when I came barreling in and bowled her over like she had done to me the last time we were in this stable house.

"Holly Hocks!"

"Juniper Berries!!!"

Juniper kissed my cheeks then pretended to bite me and said, "I'm so hungry I could just eat you; you little stinker!"

I smelled her familiar orange-blossom scent, and it made me feel happy. "Where did they take you?" I asked.

"To go get pancakes," Déjeuner chimed in with a smirk.

"Huh?" I asked.

"Long story ..." Juniper rolled her eyes as she stuffed a bran muffin in her mouth. She must have been extra hungry because she ate and ate and ate until everything they brought her was gone. She followed her meal with a big swig of juice. I watched as her throat muscles bobbed up and down guzzling the drink.

Juniper sat back with her hand over her belly and said, "Oh, maybe I shouldn't have eaten all that so quickly." A loud ***BUUUUUURRRRP*** erupted from her throat as she sheepishly exclaimed, "Excuse me, but, boy, do I feel better now!"

Begonia was noticeably quiet. She was not the kind of girl to be so silent. She was sitting on the hay covered floor, looking down, and half-heartedly twiddling a piece of hay between her thumb and fingers.

"Is there something the matter, Begonia?" I asked.

She breathed, hemmed, and hawed. "I'm just tired and ready to go home," she sulked.

Evidently Begonia was bored. She was a tad dramatic whenever she wasn't being entertained.

"I think we're all ready to go home," Déjeuner said.

"You can say that again!" Juniper huffed.

"I think we're all ready to go home," Déjeuner said again.

"You know what I'm ready to do?" I asked while standing up.

"What?" they all asked.

"Square dance!" I offered Begonia my outstretched elbow. After a wink and a click of my tongue, she reluctantly got up and we started singing and dancing.

"Grab your partner by the hand!
Dance together and make it grand!

Can't go now till we have some fun,
pound the ground till the day is done."

Juniper grabbed Déjeuner's hand as we danced and danced ...

"It's right by right by wrong you go,
it's home little gal and do-si-do.
This may be the last time, I don't know,
and oh by gosh and oh by Joe."

... until we all fell down.

Begonia's face brightened up to say the least. All of our faces were bright with glee. This stable house was the perfect setting for a good old-fashioned square dance.

"I have an idea!" Begonia stated.

"What?" I asked.

"We should square dance in the talent competition!" Her face was practically illuminated with the thought of our performance. But I knew I wouldn't be able to do anything.

"I already promised Coriander I would do something with him," I said.

Begonia's face went from glee to suspicion. Apparently she still liked him, and I wasn't supposed to do *ANYTHING* with him. Begonia crossed her arms and sulked again.

"What talent are you guys going to do?" Déjeuner asked.

I didn't know how to answer her because we weren't actually going to perform so I said the first thing that came into my head, "It's a surprise!"

CHAPTER 40
The Great Hair Extraction

Star Day was rapidly approaching. I could sense the excitement in the atmosphere. Groups of kids were found in corners or in rooms practicing their acts. It was exciting. I watched as kids directed one another, argued, then made up. Some kids were bossy, others were sadly untalented, while some were obviously gifted. Watching everyone's efforts made me excited to see the show. Would I be able to see the show?

Last year, I was trapped in THE DUNGEON missing all of the festivities except for the grand finale—the conjunction of Jupiter, Venus, and Regulus which formed The Star of Panivita. I wondered if we would have to go to the mausoleum again to witness The Solar Cross. I would not miss this occasion for anything.

I decided to be on my best behavior. I could take no chances … sounds easy, right? *WRONG!!!*

There I was sitting in Miss Guide's class, minding my own business when Thistle came in and sat behind me. I looked around thinking, *why'd she have to sit there when there were plenty of other seats available*? Nettle walked in and sat down next to Thistle … *of course*. I heard them sniggering. I shook my head at their immaturity.

Miss Guide called the class to order so I decided to pay attention to the teacher, instead of the jerks sitting behind me. I began to listen to the lesson when I felt one of my hairs being pulled from my scalp.

Boink!

"Ouch!" I yelped, grabbed the back of my head, and turned around. Thistle wouldn't look at me as she was pretending to know nothing about my hair being pulled.

Miss Guide halted her lesson because of my interruption then continued after I turned back around. I tried to refocus on the diagrams Miss Guide was drawing on the board when another strand of hair was plucked from my head.

"Ouch!" I yelped again. Miss Guide stared at me in a way I have never seen her glare at any student. She turned back to her board to continue her lesson. I had a hard time getting back to the lesson. After a while, I felt a blast of air that felt like a piece of gum or spit fly into the back of my head. That was it! That was enough!

"Hey!" I called out. "She spit gum in my hair!" I stood pointing to Thistle.

Miss Guide set down her chalk, walked over to me, and looked at my head. I turned to see Miss Guide shaking her head. Surely, she would send Thistle to Director Pankins to get spankings.

"Holly, if you can't keep quiet, you'll be going to see Director Pankins," Miss Guide warned.

"Me??? But she's the one who pulled *my* hairs out and spit gum in *my* hair," I said.

"There's nothing in your hair, Holly," Miss Guide said.

"Huh?" I felt around my head. It was true, there was nothing in my hair … which was a relief but also made me look a little looney to Miss Guide and the rest of the class.

Thistle would not meet my eyes as I sat back down. Everyone was glaring at me with disappointment. I couldn't help that Thistle was being a jerk, *as usual.* I started to get mad at everyone, especially Thistle. I could feel the blood boiling in my chest making its way to my head. I didn't hear a word Miss Guide had said in class. All I could think about was getting that butt-for-brains back.

Before I knew it, class was over, but Thistle wasn't done having fun. She stood up before I could then she did the old break-an-egg-on-the-top-of-the-head trick before leaving. But this time, instead of it being a phantom egg that rolled down my face, it was real yolk dribbling all over my head. I jolted up from my desk then ran after her. I could see fear in her ugly evil eyes as she ran away from me. Before I could catch her, a set of hairy arms grabbed me. I writhed and wriggled trying with all my might, but I was lifted off my feet making all my struggles useless. It was mean old Mr. Meanor, delighted with his catch.

"Well, what do we have here? I've been waitin' fer you to step outta line, you wretchin' frechin' smarmy ol' rascal. I knew it'd happen sooner er later," he said with a little too much elation. "Can't wait to see what Director Pankins has cooked up fer you," he continued as he dragged me away. Thistle poked her head around as Nettle came up beside her. They pretended to cry by rolling their fists into balls, twisting them over their eyes. Then they proceeded to laugh and point at me.

I hated them.

CHAPTER 41
ROCK 'EM SOCK 'EM

My blood was way beyond boiling as I waited in the office of Director Pankins who was taking her time to come in to punish me. Mean old Mr. Meanor didn't even offer me a rag to clean myself. I sat with my arms crossed as the egg was beginning to harden in my hair.

The door creaked open. "What's this?" Miss Pankins exclaimed after she entered. "Get this mess out of here." The director was still not put together; it was like she was just going through the motions.

"I brought this troublemaker here because she can't seem to keep 'er hands to herself," the mean old man said.

"I didn't do anything! Thistle was the one who pulled my hair, spit in it, and then cracked this egg on my head. I didn't do anything to her! She's the troublemaker, not me!"

"Is this true?" the director perked up a tad as she asked Mr. Meanor. He shrugged. "Get this Thistle in here as well. We'll get to the bottom of this. Oh, and bring an egg back with you."

He left the office. I stayed quiet, trying to calm down. Maybe the director wasn't as bad as I thought. Maybe she would be fair by punishing the real culprit by cracking an egg on Thistle's head, too. That would be so funny! We would share a good laugh, and maybe Miss Pankins would develop a softer side toward me.

"Ew," Thistle said when she came in. Mean old Mr. Meanor sat her down next to me. She still had that putrid smirk on her face. I wanted to wipe it off with my fist. She looked at me then stuck out her ugly, green tongue.

Without even thinking for one second, I stood up and clocked her right on the mouth. Her face flung back as her teeth wobbled. Fear washed over her face after my fist wiped off her cockiness.

"Ow!!! She hit me!" she squealed.

I stood over her, ready to sock her again. I uttered a bunch of words and threats that came from a place so deep in my being, even I can't repeat them. She flinched while holding her mouth. Someone grabbed me before I could do or say anymore. It all happened so fast, I wished I could have slowed down time.

The director and mean old Mr. Meanor were surprised by my slug, but the one most shocked was Thistle, who started to cry. Needless to say, our meeting was over, and we were both brought down to THE DUNGEON.

Mr. Meanor handed the raw egg to Thistle before he left.

"Whath's thisth for?" she asked.

"In case you get hungry."

"How am I thuppothed to eat it? Itsth raw!"

"Ask Holly! Sunny side up on top of your head, right?" he chuckled at his lame joke. "Holly, you can do the honors," he offered.

I grabbed the egg out of her hand then broke it on top of her head. "Hey!" she yelled but stopped when I glowered at her.

"You should know better than to waste food around here," Mr. Meanor said before he closed the heavy groaning door to THE DUNGEON.

She sulked, but I took a dollop of delight at his joke. He knew as well as I that she was a numbskull-for-brains. But I was still disappointed in myself. I had a long streak of staying out of trouble, and now I wasn't sure what would happen. I had to be out of here before the Star Day celebration.

I hated the thought of being stuck in this place, especially with *her*. She was acting so hurt by just one little punch … and one little egging … what a nincompoop! She had a rag on her mouth catching any blood that formed. I looked at my throbbing fist taking note of her snaggletooth imprint on my knuckles. Looks like I really did give her a knuckle sandwich. It never felt so good to be in such pain.

She snuck a look at me but my eyes were so constricted, I must have intimidated her because she looked away as if she was scared. Bullies … they are so dumb and weak after you stand up to them. All she had to do was leave me alone, and none of this would have happened. But because she couldn't resist being a jerk, now we were stuck in this smelly, damp, musty-pot—the butt of The Children's Horrible House.

It seemed like forever before either of us spoke. The silence became a divider in the room that separated us better than a wall. I had nothing to say to her. Above all, I wanted to hear nothing from her—especially with the spit that popped out of her mouth every time she spoke.

I calmed down some as the pain in my hand increased. My hand and I had accepted our punishment. What else could I do? My stomach had other plans, however. It was gurgling and obviously hungry. It kept making all these weird noises that I tried to cover, but as they escaped, they echoed across the walls. The sounds were getting out of hand, and, finally, Thistle could stay silent no longer. What she said was something I never expected.

"I'm thorry."

I couldn't believe my ears. Did she just apologize to me? I looked at her skeptically.

"Okay, I know you probably will never be my friend, but I'm thorry for egging you."

"Why did you do it?" I asked.

"I don't know. Nettle thought it would be funny, and thometimeth you just theem like an eathy target."

"*Eathy target*?" I mimicked her. "Do you realithe how thtupid *you* thound?"

"Hey! I have a lithp!"

"That doesn't give you the right to pick on everyone, okay! And if you lay another finger or egg on me or any one of my friends, your lisp won't be a problem for you anymore."

"What do you mean?"

I balled up my swollen fist and said, "Because I will knock all of your snaggly yellow teeth right down your smelly throat. Got it?" I started to move toward her as she scooted back.

Something in my look must have made her believe me even though I wasn't sure if I believed myself at the moment. We both returned to the silence that dwelled heavily in this dank dungeon.

Thistle breathed in and out then said, "Look, like I thaid, I know we will never be frienth, but how about we call a truthe."

"A truce?"

"Yeth. I'll leave you alone, and you leave me alone."

I wanted to say something like, *I did leave you alone or you better leave me alone*, but I didn't want to continue or escalate this situation anymore. All my anger or excitement had worn off. I certainly never wanted to be friends with Thistle or Nettle, but a truce seemed to be the best and only option.

"Okay, truce."

If only it could be so, I hoped.

CHAPTER 42

IDEAS, ANYONE?

Coriander was walking through the hallway when Begonia spotted him. He was looking for Holly so they could be prepared for the next evening's events.

"Hi Coriander, whatcha doin'?" Begonia asked.

"Just looking for Holly, have you seen her?"

"Not recently. You two need to practice?"

"Practice what?"

"For the talent show. Holly said you guys were doing something together for the talent show."

At first Coriander didn't know what Begonia was talking about but then caught on. "Oh yeah! That's right … we are!"

Begonia put on a sneaky expression and asked, "Can you tell me what it is?"

Coriander racked his brain, widened his eyes, then said, "It's a surprise!"

"Fiddlesticks! That's the same thing she said."

Coriander gave Begonia a twinkle that made her slightly swoon.

"Hey, if you find Holly, tell her that I already fed Cookie, Eenie, Meenie, Miney, and Moe," Begonia counted on her fingers.

Coriander's confused brows scrunched.

"The hamsters," Begonia clarified.

"Oh, okay, I'll tell her."

Clover and the twins walked up and Staniel asked, "Tell who what?"

Coriander was just about to walk away, but something made him stay for this meeting.

"Holly … I fed her hamsters," Begonia filled them in.

"Oh that's good because she definitely can't feed them right now," Clover said.

"What do you mean?" Begonia asked.

"Didn't you hear?" Danley asked.

"Hear about what?" Coriander jumped into the conversation.

"Holly did somethin' to Thistle aftah Thistle egged her, and now they are in THE DUNGEON," Clover informed everyone.

"What did Holly do?" Begonia asked.

"I heard she punched Thistle," Clover said in a voice filled with excitement.

"Are you for real?" Begonia's eyes bugged out.

"That's what I heard, but I'm not sure. I didn't see it with my own eyes," Clover said.

"Don't you mean eye?" Staniel teased.

"Hardy har har … so funny," Clover shook her head and gave Staniel's arm a little punch.

While Staniel rubbed his arm, Coriander scooted away trying to go unnoticed, but the group of kids followed him. He realized he wouldn't be able to shake them off so he decided to make the best of the situation.

They walked toward THE DUNGEON, but when they came to the turn, mean old Mr. Meanor and Mr. Ree were standing guard. No one was going to get past those two. The group of kids continued along as if they headed elsewhere. As soon as they were far enough away, they regrouped.

"What's the plan?" Danley asked.

Coriander thought a second then said, "As of now, there is no plan."

"That's not a good plan," Staniel said.

"That's because it isn't one yet, duh," Begonia chimed in to take some pressure off Coriander.

"Any ideas, anyone?" Clover asked.

"Hmmm … Nope … Not a one," Danley pondered.

"Well, since we are not going anywhere here. I think I'll catch you guys later," Coriander tried to make his escape.

"Yeah, we'll catch you guys later," Begonia walked off with Coriander but he preferred to go alone.

"Actually, Begonia would you mind, I have to use the bathroom."

"Oh, sorry," she said as Coriander walked away.

CHAPTER 43
Time Stands Still

Hours stalled to a pace so slow that if jumping through time were possible, this was the opportune moment. We stayed in THE DUNGEON for who knows how long before Major Whoopins and Mr. Ree came in to let us out. My eyes had to adjust to so much light as we emerged from the darkness. Even though we were free, our punishment was not over. We had to work together by doing heaps and heaps of dirty laundry. If you asked me, though, this was way better than doing loads and loads of dirty dishes but not better than cleaning dirty toilets … yes, we had to clean dirty toilets.

I would have rather received a bunch of paddles over cleaning these stinky toilets. Together we folded sheets, towels, uniforms, and other necessaries. We scrubbed, swished, swashed, and wiped toilets until they sparkled while Mr. Ree stood guard making sure we did it right.

We did this awful, repetitious, punishing activity until dark. Thankfully, I was finally able to clean myself. The egg yolk had been glued to my head all day. It never felt so good to get myself so squeaky. The warm shower was exactly what I needed before I crawled into my newly laundered sheets.

Even though the day had gone horribly wrong, it felt fabulous to feel so comforted inside these fresh linens. I twisted around under the covers until I found the softest spot. They smelled like summertime and soap. I drifted off to sleep with those lulling scents taking me to dreamland.

I had a million dreams that night but only one that I could clearly remember. I dreamed that I missed the entire Star Day celebration. When I woke up inside my dream, no one was here anymore. I was all alone at The Children's Horrible House. I ran around looking for everyone, but the house was empty. I called out and listened for a reply but none came. I closed my eyes to yell as loudly as possible, but my voice made no sound. When I opened my eyes, the house was gone. I was standing in the spot where the horrible house used to be. There was nothing left and no trace that it had ever been there. I ran toward the horrible growing garden which promptly picked me up and swallowed me whole.

I woke up for real with sweat dripping from my stiff aching body. I looked around the dark shadowy house. Quietly, the mansion stood steadfast and strong as everyone else slept soundly. I checked on Déjeuner and Begonia but saw that Déjeuner's bunk was empty. Where was she at this time of night? Maybe she was with Juniper in the stable house. Those two were inseparable.

After going back and forth, my eyelids became heavier before I fell back to sleep. I didn't wake up until late morning while everyone was chattering away about the day's activities. It was Star Day! This time I was not in THE DUNGEON or trapped in The Hanging Cage. I would do anything to make sure I was part of the festivities.

Breakfast was weird. It was weird because it was good and by *good* I mean delicious. We had buttery French toast, syrupy sausages, and fried cinnamon apples. Begonia slurped her syrup like it was the tastiest confection on Earth. The twins tried bargaining with everyone to share with them, but no one would give up their goodies. Clover hovered so closely to her food, nobody had a chance to take any. Déjeuner was still missing. She had to still be with Juniper, I truly hoped. And Coriander … well, who knew?

I ate every morsel, drip, and crumb. I thought about licking the plate but thought that might not be the best idea. Staniel and Danley however, did not show such constraint. Round plates moved up and down in front of their faces while their mouths vacuumed up the remnants.

After morning work, everyone was allowed to rehearse their acts for the talent show. It was fun watching as everyone came together to bond or fight over their performance. I envied the more talented performers, wishing I had a real talent to share. But I was not good at anything that belonged on stage.

The afternoon was filled with fun and laughter. We had relay races and egg tosses where I did not get covered in yolk, thankfully. There were sack races, tug-o-war, and hula hoop competitions—which as it turns out, I was good at. I could swirl that hoop around for hours. I totally beat everyone … yay me!

Just as I was feeling extra good about myself, Coriander approached me to say, "It's almost time … stay nearby."

I was feeling good about my victory. I wasn't ready to get serious. I wanted more fun. It was like a carnival here. We walked around grabbing popcorn and snow cones while watching all the kids compete just for fun. In the distance, I spotted the horrible growing garden on the other side of the field. It was getting much too big and scary looking.

When the whistle blew, everyone stopped what they were doing then settled into the theater for the talent competition. The six of us took up the greater section of a row. The theater was a room that made you feel special just to be inside it. It was so fancy, ornate, and still … so still, it felt quiet as a coffin. The seats were plush, padded, and covered in blanket-soft velvet. I kept running my hands back and forth watching the colors change with each swipe—plus, it was soft on my hands.

When the curtain opened, a bright spotlight centered on the stage. There were two kids dressed in fancy getups. When the big band music started, their feet began to tip and tap all over the stage, thrilling the excited audience. They were obviously very talented. When they were finished, I thought they would win the competition for sure—until the next act.

Two sets of boys dressed in baggy checkered pants, yellow puffy jackets, and high-top sneakers began to move like robots as the beat dropped. Their movements were so realistic; it was like they really were robots until they started breakdancing like the kids I saw back at Compass Academy. Now I wasn't sure who would win because they were both so good.

I knew who wouldn't win though. A tall black-haired girl wearing a red dress and thick-framed glasses caught a bad case of stage fright. When the spotlight hit her, she froze. I heard some uncomfortable throat clearings while a couple of people tried to nudge her, but she was stiff. Eventually, she had to be pulled from the stage. I felt bad for her but also curious about what we missed in not seeing her performance. What if it was spectacular? Guess we'll never know.

Thankfully, the crowd's favorite came next. Kamut, the kid from Miss Guide's class used his armpits to make fart noises in rhythm to *Superman's* theme song. I loved Superman!

He was challenged by another kid who burped the capital cities of all fifty states. At the end of the performance, the student took off a baseball cap revealing that she was a girl. Surprise! A burping girl!

After a few more acts, Coriander got up to "use the restroom" … or at least that was how it was supposed to appear. The next act walked onto the unlit stage. Suspenseful music began to play, the spotlight illuminated, then instead of a magician pulling a rabbit out of a hat, a kid inside a giant bunny costume pulled a small stuffed magician out of a black top hat! How clever I thought … it was so good that I lost track of time until a loud crunchy boom sent everyonc into alcrt.

We all thought it was part of the show, but when it happened again, it shook the entire house to its foundation. This time we knew something was not right. The house started to shake uncontrollably causing all the kids to scatter. Everyone ran. I went to a window only to see the pulsing radioactive-looking vines covering everything—I could not see out. Where was Coriander? I had to find him.

CHAPTER 44
IRRESISTIBLE SUMMONS

The director wasn't sure if it came from inside her own head but with all the hubbub and excitement during the talent show, she still heard her mother's voice loud and clear. She tried to ignore it, thinking that she was potentially going crazy after all those sleepless nights. She feared that she was truly coming undone—losing her sanity. She just wanted to find peace at this point. Nothing was worth the anguish from which her soul was suffering. It was like she was becoming divided or mutating.

Perhaps she was going through a metamorphosis much like the glowing garden had gone from a peaceful night-blooming sanctuary (which she hadn't truly appreciated enough until it was gone), to this horrible monster of a garden that was taking over, suffocating everything in its path. A vibration from the ground was shaking the house. Maybe it was the loud music from the talent show. She couldn't watch anymore because her head was pounding with the loud music. She needed some fresh air before she suffocated within the walls of her horrible house.

Without a thought as to where she was heading, Sirius found herself in front of the opalescent ferocious garden, which had grown out of control. It had practically covered the entire house in its creeping monstrous vines. She stood still, unsure of what to do when enticing tentacles signaled for her to enter. The last time she was within its borders, it tried to digest her. What might it do now? The garden opened for her, inviting her within its sanctum. Under some kind of hypnotic trance, she entered while the entity closed around her.

Vines pushed her deeper and deeper until she came to a specific spot. In the ground was a shadow of a circle marked with the solar cross. The garden pushed her to stand atop the symbol. She looked up into the barely visible sky to see the same shape above her. She stood between the solar cross in the sky and the one etched into earth. Just as she blinked her eyes, the ground opened up with a boom, swallowing the director whole.

CHAPTER 45
THE GREAT RESCUE

The five of us ran outside. The growing garden climbed the sides of the house like King Kong clinging to the buildings in New York City. The gargantuan growth had gotten so big, it looked like it was trying to swallow The Children's Horrible House. I heard the rush of kids clambering out of the house while mayhem ensued. From within the garden, a flock of iridescent doves flew in a spiral up toward the sky then scattered in every direction. I wasn't sure which way to go until I felt a tug on my arm and saw Coriander holding me. His face set and sure, signaled for all of us to follow him.

While everyone skittered away from the garden, we raced into it. The deeper we went, less of the house could be seen. A tunnel of cosmic colors sparkled as we plodded through a swirling vortex that was aggressively gaining more horrifying growth.

"Where is it?" Coriander asked.

"What?" I wondered.

"The tomb. Hawthorne North Star's tomb, where did it go?"

"Maybe it's just been overrun by all these plants," Clover suggested as a vine was crawling over her shoulders.

"Let's keep going. It's probably deeper than we remember."

A loud creak and a crash came from a window being broken under the strength of the strangling garden. Oh no! It sounded like the house was beginning to crumble.

"Guys! I'll be right back," I called as I ran back toward the house.

"Where are you going?" Coriander called.

"I have to get Cookie and her babies!"

"I'm coming too," Begonia ran after me.

We bobbled against the flow of kids running out before jogging up the stairs into my dormitory. There she was! Cookie was huddled with her babies, keeping them safe. I grabbed the cage. We started to walk back out when I heard a familiar meow coming from the air vents. It was Copper, Miss Judge's kitty! I had to rescue him too!

"Here, you take Cookie and her babies, and I'll go get Copper," I told Begonia. The house creaked and groaned while Begonia's eyes grew into saucers of concern.

"You sure?" she asked.

"Yes! Go!"

She turned to go while I ran up the forever flights of stairs then down the long dark hallways. Finally, I pulled open the library's double doors. I walked in. After a couple of seconds, I heard his meowing but couldn't find him.

"Copper! Copper!" I called then listened for his meow.

"Meow … Meeeeoooww," his calls got louder. I walked through the aisles. I finally found the wall of books from where his meows were coming. I wasn't sure what to do. I heard him meow loudly again which made me think that perhaps he was behind the books.

I pulled them out and threw them on the floor (exactly what you're NOT supposed to do with books). I repeated tossing the books until I grabbed one tiny, flimsy-looking pamphlet that opened up a dark hidden chamber.

I walked inside, looked up, then saw Copper pacing on top of a circular staircase.

"Hi there, little kitty! C'mon! Let's go!" I said urgently.

He slithered around, then he must have gotten spooked by another window being crunched because he quickly bounded down the stairs past me. I tried to keep up with him as he raced to the double doors. I opened them for us before he ran through the hallways like a cheetah. I didn't see him again until I was coming around the bend as he was dashing outside. When I finally made it to the doorway, I watched his back legs bounce him into the thicket of woods. He was much safer out there.

It had become much darker as the sun was shadowed by the moon's eclipse. The sky was making strange shapes and colors that moved around like paint strokes coming to life by an invisible artist. I felt like I had seen lights like this before but only in pictures. I walked slowly gazing up until I found everyone close to where I had left them last.

They were all staring at a strange shape in the ground. It was big and round, and looked mushy. Coriander walked over to it, stepped inside, and was immediately gobbled up by the ground. Begonia's eyes bugged out. My eyes must have done the same thing. We looked at each other, shocked by Coriander's disappearance. I couldn't let him be gobbled up by the ground all alone.

I hopped inside the circle then looked up into the sky for one unforgettable moment. I caught a brief flash of the solar cross around the eclipsed sun as I was taken down within the subterranean dirt. A strange sensation followed. Bolts of neon-colored electricity exploded all around me. My vision was blurred by the quickness of blasts that zoomed by. Pulses of heat struck my body but left me unharmed. It was as if I was being transported through lightening protected by the ground that had swallowed me.

Time turned into something else. It was like a black hole or a vacuum that sucked the air right out of my lungs. When my body stopped hurdling through wherever I was, everything else stopped too.

CHAPTER 46
BURIED ALIVE

Sirius Pankins lay on the ground surrounded by the bright faceted crystals that beamed luminescence to the twinkling lights in the garden above it. The hidden cave was under the whole estate. Little did Hawthorne North Star know at first what lay hundreds of feet beneath the terrain of his noble house. But one person knew. Actually, her people had known about its power for centuries but they never entered it. Revelations interpreted by the elders foretold of its legacy that would be passed down through the generations. But the fruition of the prophesy always seemed so far away until now. Everything in space and time was coming into alignment, not just on a physical level—metaphysically as well.

"Come to me, my daughter," an echoing voice spoke from within the mirror. The shadow of someone else was lurking within the cavern and walked up to the encrusted mirror. What the lurker saw almost caused the figure to faint.

"Steady! My, my … well look at you!" an echoing voice said

from within the mirror. "Is that you, Willow?"

Willow nodded, too shocked to speak. "My Willow Faint Star, you are the spitting image of your grandmother," Hawthorne North Star said to his daughter.

Willow could hardly believe her eyes. She could not remember ever actually seeing her father, but now they were face to face. Tears rolled down her cheeks. She could hardly think. "How is this possible? I thought you were … were …"

"Dead?" he asked.

She had trouble saying the word and even more difficulty understanding the possibility of it being untrue.

"Yes."

In a deep soothing drawl, Hawthorne attempted to explain his state. "Well, that's hard to define now, dear. Death is a tricky concept. You see, if I were on the other side of this mirror, standing where you are, I would most certainly be … um … not alive but here, in The Meadow, I can live forever."

Willow was puzzled. What did he mean by The Meadow? She looked behind him and saw a multitude of people and animals prancing joyfully around while others sat contemplatively.

"So, you never died … you just left … me," she deduced.

"I never technically died, but I also never intended to leave you. I came here to find someone."

"Sings-in-the-Meadow?" Willow said with accusations sprinkled over the woman's name.

Hawthorne cleared his throat and said, "Yes, that is right."

Willow became quiet. Her emotions bounced in every direction leading her to feel angry, sad, joyful, but, mostly, confused.

"Did you find her?"

"I did, yes."

"Soooo, you guys can live happily ever after," she said in mocking tone.

"We are very happy but not together. You see, in The Meadow we are free from that kind of love. We are Love." He could tell she wanted a more in-depth, personal explanation. "Willow, I was very much in love with your mother. When I lost her, Sings-in-the-Meadow taught me about things I had never thought were possible. It was an awakening. She told me about unbelievable things, and honestly, it took me until she had gone for me to actually believe her. After Sings-in-the-Meadow left, I felt more alone than ever. I wanted to die but before I did, I came here one evening and found her. I was able to cross over. We have been trying to reach you ever since. Willow, this is the last time you can enter through this portal. After tonight no one knows when it will be open again. Now is your only chance."

She heard the earnestness in his tone and thought about everything she had been through to finally see this day. Nothing is ever how you picture it, but this was definitely miraculous. Then he said something that made her final decision.

"Oh, and I also found the rest of our family. Would you like to see them?"

Willow heard his words but found them to be verging upon the unfathomable. How was it possible? Of course she wanted to see them. "Yes!"

"Come, I'll take you to them," Hawthorne said.

"How?"

"Climb into here," Hawthorne signaled for her to crawl through the mirror.

Willow put her hand on the crusted mirror and the tips of her fingers sunk within the silver.

"Stop!" Reed called out before Willow turned around.

"If you go in, you can never return. You will remain there eternally," Reed warned.

"Where?" Sirius surprised everyone when she spoke from behind them. Willow and Reed both turned to see her walking toward the mirror.

"The Meadow," Reed said.

"How do you know about this place?" Willow asked Reed.

"Because I was very tempted to go there."

"Why didn't you?"

"Because I had some unfinished business that I wasn't aware of … until recently."

"What?"

"My daughter."

"You have a daughter?" the director asked.

"Yes," Reed said. "Saffron, you are my daughter."

Sirius was stunned and could not react as one might think, hope, or fathom. She would not and could not believe him. Her father was Hawthorne North Star. That is what she believed—what she would prefer to believe and would always believe.

Everyone was stunned except for the images within the mirror. A voice soft and sweet spoke in a language no one understood. Sings-in-the-Meadow danced around, stomped, and twirled in a show of happiness.

In broken English she spoke, "Daughter, my radiant light, please come. Home, Meadow waits for you. You home. Come … me … inside." Her eyes lit up as something ignited their spark. As if she was hypnotized, Sirius's eyes reflected the same radiance as her mother's. Sings-in-the-Meadow gestured for Sirius to enter the glass.

Reed was transfixed. The love of his life stood before him. He heard her vexing voice, but she didn't call out to him. She had summoned only their daughter, Saffron. The note inside the doll explained everything but left him with more questions. It delighted him to see Sings-in-the-Meadow but broke his heart especially since she did not acknowledge him. He still loved her. But her love was not like his. Her love would always be with her people, and Saffron was most evidently hers.

Without thinking of treasure or anything material, Sirius placed her hands on the mirror.

"Saffron wait! Please tell her," he pleaded with Sings-in-the-Meadow.

Sings-in-the-Meadow looked into Reed Trustworthy's eyes and said, "You are good man. Come with to Meadow," she spoke words he wanted to hear but knew what would happen if he listened.

"Saffron if you go inside, you can never return. You will surely die," he warned.

"Live forever in Meadow," Sings-in-the-Meadow rebutted.

Sirius saw what she had been looking for for years … the missing piece within her puzzling soul. On the other side of the mirror, she found peace, sanity, her long lost feeling of complete love, and most valuable treasure. The glimpses she had previously captured of this moment prepared her for what she truly wanted. Her mother being whole, alive, and together on the other side of the glass brought her back to the Saffron Radiant Star she was born to be. And suddenly, all the ephemera that had passed as Director Sirius Pankins seemed to never have occurred—to be lost in a place of time and space.

Without hesitation, she reached for the mirror as the crystals heated up singeing her hands right before she leaped inside. Everything began to quake and shudder. A shimmery fine dust fell from the walls and ceiling. Reed and Willow grabbed onto the closest stable object. In a flash Saffron Radiant Star, for a period of time known as Director Sirius Pankins, was gone.

"No!" Reed called out as his fists clenched, trying to hold on to something that couldn't be restrained.

Willow stood stunned. She had just witnessed a live person being sucked inside a crystal-crusted mirror. She watched as Reed stood bereft. He aged by a few decades instantly.

Chapter 47
The Power Within

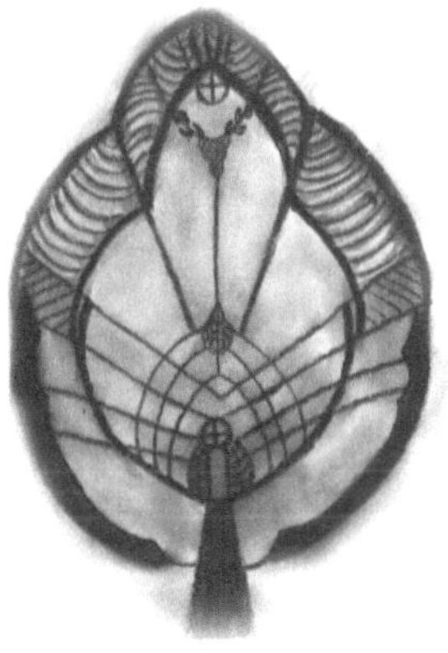

The ground shook and sputtered until I finally awoke to Miss Judge staring into a mirror while Mr. Trustworthy was slumped over his knees with despair hopelessly drowning his face.

"Let's go!" Miss Judge whispered in a child-like tone. "This may be our only chance, Reed. This is what I have been waiting for my whole life. Tonight is the only night we can get through."

Reed didn't move at all. Miss Judge tried more to convince him. "I've been studying this exclusively for years. You see … on the eve of the Solar Cross, through the power of these crystals and this geological hotspot, we can travel through space and time, access another dimension—The Meadow."

"I have nowhere," he said sadly.

"We have there." Willow pointed to the mirror. He looked up with tears streaming down his face. He shook his head then covered his face. Why was he so upset? I wondered.

Voices coming from the mirror took his attention while a look of surrender invaded his features. Miss Judge placed her hands on his hands and brought him before the looking glass.

"Go … I'll be right behind you," she said.

The rumbling that ensued was bound to make the entire cave collapse. In two flashes, I was all alone. What just happened? Was what I had just seen possible? Why didn't I call out? Why didn't I stop them? For some reason, I froze. What was inside that mirror? Was that where the treasure was hidden?

I walked over to it and saw a large flower-filled meadow. In the sky above it, a rainbow arched across, falling into white billowing clouds. A butterfly flickered its colorful wings as a cute puppy dog chased it. Wait a second … that puppy dog looked familiar. I adjusted my eyes to make sure they wouldn't lie to me. Considering how full my eyes were with tears, I couldn't detect any deception.

Could it be him? *Could it*? It was! It was Falafel! My most cutest, wonderful, playful, sweet, howling, one blue-eyed, one brown-eyed puppy dog. He looked so happy!!! Just like Ginger told me he would be!

"Falafel!" I called out. He immediately stopped chasing the insect and ran toward me with his tongue hanging out of the side of his mouth. He came up to the glass then sat before me letting out a soft howl.

"Owwwwwwllll."

"Owwwwwwllll," I howled back with tears streaming down my cheeks. He signaled that he wanted me to pet him like I always had before. He got on his side wanting me to scratch the side of his belly so he could kick around like he was starting a motorcycle. As I reached in, the ground shook. My hands began to burn. My whole body began to get sucked into a black hole. My vision was gone when suddenly everything shattered.

I fell back onto the hard spiky ground, briefly catching a glimpse of Coriander holding a long club. I guarded my head and closed my eyes as shards of crystals fell all around me. After the dust settled, I glanced up to the crystal-crusted mirror seeing only a shallow hole.

"Hey, why did you do that?" I bawled to Coriander, but there was no time for him to reply. A bunch of jagged crystals fell from the ceiling coming much too close to stabbing me. He grabbed me then forced me to run ahead of him. The rumbling and shaking that had occurred earlier was nothing compared to what was happening now. The crystal cave was crumbling around us. How would we get out? We needed help, now! I began to panic and wished that someone would come save us.

Coriander found the way that we had used before, but it was rapidly being closed off by giant falling crystalline javelins. A wall of the kid-killing jewels fell, trapping the two of us. The vibration was so strong it tickled my ears. I had no time to scratch them; I was trying to think of a way to save our lives.

Coriander and I looked at one another in a way we had never before expressed. This was it. We were about to be goners, history, worm food. I breathed hard as nervous sweat trickled down my face.

"What are we going to do? What are we going to do?" I asked, beginning to panic. Coriander grabbed my hand and said, "Holly, you're my best friend and you always will be. If we don't make it out of here, I want you to know that."

"I know … and ditto," I said—my voice thumping with the ground and my beating heart.

Coriander wasn't the type to get all mushy and neither was I, but this could possibly be the last time we would see each other on this side of life. He held out his hands. I put my head on his shoulder, squeezed his hand, and embraced him as we accepted our doomed fate.

CHAPTER 48
SOMETHIN' AIN'T RIGHT

The twins, Begonia, and Clover saw the ground swallow Coriander before ingesting Holly. When they tried to follow them, they were apprehended by Mr. Meanor and Mr. Ree who, instead of taking them back into the crumbling horrible house, took them to the smelly stable house. After they were inside, Begonia expected to find Juniper and Déjeuner, but there were so many kids, it was next to impossible to find them.

"What should we do with these rotten, pokin', pesky kids?" Mr. Meanor asked the major.

"We wait fo' word from the director. I done told ya'll. Right now we just need to make sure all these kids is safe," Major Whoopins said. "But now, ya'll need to get back out there and find if there are anymo' missin' kids 'sides Déjeuner Buffet, Holly Spinatsch, and Coriander Oats." He flipped through pages of names on his clipboard with most of them checked off … except for those three.

In the back of the major's mind, he was sure Juniper, Holly's sister, was still here, *sneakin' around lookin' fo' her sister.* He couldn't blame her. What big sister wouldn't protect their younger sibling? Still, he wanted to make sure that she and Déjeuner were safe considering all the danger that was surrounding the house. Last he knew, it looked like that crazy over-growing garden was taking over everything, —the house included. It wasn't just your average healthy green space; this was a monster from another universe gobbling up everything in its path.

The ground convulsed gathering more force with each quake. All the kids screamed as hay drifted down from the loft. The major grabbed hold of one of the beams until the shaking subsided. A stray thought crept into his mind … *where was Miss Pankins*? He had never worried for her before because she was always so commanding, but something felt odd.

Major Whoopins looked around and saw Miss Treetment tending to some wounds while Miss Shapen walked slowly next to Hugh Mungus who was sweeping up the fallen hay. The lunch ladies were walking around squawking like ostriches. Most of the staff was accounted for … except for Miss Pankins, Miss Judge, and Mr. Reed Trustworthy.

The major walked over to Miss Spelling who was keeping the kids occupied with a lesson on earthquakes as the ground continued to tremble. He asked her if she and the other teachers would keep an eye on everyone while he went out to go look for the director.

"Absolutely Major, but do be careful!" Miss Spelling warned as an aftershock jiggled the building. The kids were wide-eyed and befuddled as to what was occurring. They mumbled amongst themselves, but all in all, remained hushed by the cataclysmic events.

Major Whoopins stepped out into the night air. His gaze

immediately went up to the firmament which was eerily making a rainbow of colors in the night sky while blasts of thunder grumbled.

The obvious stars twinkled before he saluted them in return. His mission continued as he searched for Miss Pankins and whomever else he might find.

CHAPTER 49
HEARING AND SHAKING

Before the rush of kids came through the doors of the stable house, Déjeuner instinctually picked up on Holly's cry for help. Something compelled her to go investigate. Finding her was the issue.

"Juniper, Holly needs our help. She's stuck," Déjeuner said anxiously.

"Let's go!" Juniper was ready to rescue. "Where is she?"

"That, I'm not sure of …" Déjeuner bit her lip. "Hold on, let me think." She put her hands up to her head and concentrated on the direction of Holly's voice. At first it was undetectable with all the shaking going on. In between tremors, the silence produced a source.

"She's that way." Déjeuner pointed to the back of the stable house.

Juniper thought Déjeuner's instinct must be wrong because there was nothing back there. "I don't think anything is back there."

"Just follow me," the sureness in Déjeuner's voice led Juniper to cast her doubt aside. Usually someone led Déjeuener, but she was able to follow Holly's voice that signaled to her from another wavelength.

"Why did we stop?" Déjeuner asked.

"Because there is a door here."

"Well, open it."

Juniper warned, "It's covered in cobwebs."

Déjeuner used her extra-long sleeve to wipe them off. Juniper felt a little dumb to be intimidated by invisible spiders but regained her valiancy by opening the creaking hatch. A black tunnel met them on the other side of the door. It did not look inviting. Juniper imagined rats, cave crickets, and spiders crawling everywhere.

"I don't think Holly is in here," Juniper hoped.

"She's not in here, but this is how we find her," Déjeuner said.

"Great," Juniper whispered.

Déjeuner's physical sight had never worked fully, but her sixth sense never let her down. She pushed Juniper inside the tunnel, and together they tiptoed deeper and deeper until the walls started to glow. The faceted stones were mesmerizing and grew larger with each step.

When the ground shook, it knocked the two girls off their feet. This was not the ideal place to be when an earthquake decided to shake everything.

"I think we better get out of here!" Juniper warned.

"Wait! I hear her! She's just over there. "Holly! Holly! Can you hear me?" Déjeuner called.

CHAPTER 50
FOLLOWING VOICES

The moment I had given up hope, I heard the sweet, wonderful, gracious sound of angels calling my name. They were coming to take me home. Wait! I was not ready to go to heaven yet. I still had so many things to do! I needed to win a real BMX race, meet Superman, kiss him, beat up Nettle, and find the hidden treasure. I couldn't die yet, I tried to telepathically explain all this to the angels.

"You're not going to die Holly! It's us, Juniper and Déjeuner. Can you hear me?"

"Yes! I can hear you!"

Déjeuner's voice calling out for me was the best thing I'd heard all day!

"Follow my voice!" she called.

Coriander and I scuttled over closer to the source. "Say something else!" I called.

"Yodel ay he hoo!" Déjeuner yodeled.

We got as far as we could before we were stuck behind a wall of a giant fallen crystal. I could see their silhouettes through the foggy gem. We were so close yet so far from safety, especially when a powerful blast invaded the tunnel causing our blockage to come dislodged. In a flash, Coriander hoisted me over the top then leaped over after. Juniper grabbed me, gave me a big hug, then turned to Coriander, and laid a big one on him too.

"Enough with all the mush! Let's get out of here!" Déjeuner called before another blast looked to take down the entire cavern behind us. Everything was caving in. We were about to be buried alive. We ran as the tunnel was buckling behind us while it also stretched infinitely in front of us. I ran out of breath when I tumbled and scraped my knees. Coriander lifted me up then put my arm over his shoulder. We limped the rest of the way to the hatch, but once again it was jammed. With Coriander's boyish yet manly strength, he barreled it open just in time. But we still weren't safe.

CHAPTER 51
LOOKIN' AND LEAVIN'

Major Whoopins went to find the missing kids as well as the unaccounted for staff, but he was met by Mr. Ree and Mr. Meanor running toward him with looks of terror washed over their faces.

"What's goin' on?"

"We have to get outta here, man! This whole place is about to blow!"

"What do y'all mean?" Major Whoopins couldn't simply take their word, he had to see for himself. He rushed into the brewing storm that resembled the darkness of a twisting tornado but held the trembling of an earthquake.

The sky was blacked out, not by clouds or wind, but by the garden that had completely overtaken everything in its path. He could hear the house being slowly ripped apart. Glass shattered, beams buckled, and walls collapsed. The garden was eating The Children's Horrible House. With each bite, it grew more ferocious and frightening. And it was getting closer and closer. He had seen enough.

Major Whoppins turned to order the men to get the buses ready to move out. Mr. Ree and Mr. Meanor surprised him when he found them standing right behind him.

"Let's go get them buses, drive 'em to the stable house, then load up those kids. We gotta get 'em home safely," Major Whoopins yelled over the storm.

He sprang over and hopped inside his favorite bus. He turned the key, but nothing happened. Now was not the time for the buses to play around by not starting. He pumped the gas pedal and checked the lights to see if the battery was dead, but everything seemed in order.

"C'mon Betsy! Be a good bus!" Major Whoopins coaxed by petting the dashboard nicely. After a few more sputtering turns of the ignition, the bus roared to a steady rumble then headed for a big pickup.

The folding doors flew open. The three men faced a sea of kids all looking at them with wide-stretched scared eyes.

"Alright now! Everyone load up!" There was no time for detailed explanations or instructions. All the orders that these kids had been getting during the time they were here were finally used for good because they listened. One by one, in an orderly fashion, the kids loaded onto the buses.

Clover, Begonia, and the twins hesitated. They wouldn't get on those buses until they found the rest of the crew. Begonia looked down at the hamsters and told them not to worry even though she grew extra worried waiting for Holly and Coriander. She began to panic when Miss Shapen and Mr. Mungus were corralling them from behind.

"What's the holdup? Don't cha wanna go home?" Miss Shapen

snarled but then looked over at Mr. Mungus and asked, "Honey, I never thought about it till now, but where is our home?" A look of puzzlement and concern flattened over her features.

"Wherever I'm with you is home, honey." He held her jiggly arms and kissed the top of her netted head.

"Awe! My Hughy Mungy Bungy," she said in a weird childish voice that made the kids giggle in the face of imminent doom. The ground quaked so intensely, it felt like the foundation of the stable house was forever compromised.

Begonia, Clover, and the twins began to panic. They looked around as the kids boarded the buses. It would be their turn soon, but they couldn't leave knowing the rest of the gang was left behind.

"Let's go! Let's go!" Major Whoopins yelled. He looked at the sky and knew their time was almost up. "Y'all need to move!"

The kids had no choice; they had to board the bus without their friends. They took their seats and stared out the rainbow-colored windows hoping to spot Holly, Coriander, Juniper, and Déjeuner. Everyone else was on the bus when the doors began to close.

CHAPTER 52
The Escape

Coriander closed the rattling door behind us. The building shook so violently, it, too, was about to come down. We ran for the open stable doors. Juniper tripped on a rope then fell to the ground, scraping her elbows. What was wrong with us? It was like had we turned into crazy klutzes all of the sudden. Coriander went to lift her up but she shook him off, limping quickly on her own. I looked outside watching the bus's bi-fold door closing.

"Wait!" we screamed.

"Wait!"

"Wait for us!" I called, practically out of breath.

Clover, the twins, and Begonia must have called out to get the driver to reopen the doors because they were right there at the threshold waiting for us as we hopped up and in. Without waiting for us to take our seats, Major Whoopins floored the gas pedal, thrusting us in a pile of kids to the back of the bus. After we scrambled for seats, we turned around and watched as the ground swallowed everything … and by everything, I mean, the stable house, The Children's Horrible House, and that crazy horrible growing garden.

Strange, yet entirely beautiful … in the wake of disaster, a burst of brilliant blue butterflies emerged from the cloud of dust. They circled around and around then dissolved up into the sky like a retreating twisting tornado finished with its destruction. All that was left was a gentle rolling meadow filled with yellow grass—much like the meadow that appeared in *Sage Themes* and the mirror inside the crystal cave.

I recalled the vision I had seen while looking in the old leather book—the vision I relayed to Sirius Pankins. Before me was a wild meadow—how it must have appeared prior to when the house was built—a perfect place for bison to roam. I would never have predicted that these *catastrophic*, (I now knew how to use that word in a sentence), events would happen to this place.

I was sad. I had grown to cherish the horrible house in all its creepiness. It was the fanciest, scariest, shiver-inducing, mysterious house ever. I would miss it and think of it fondly even if there was no treasure.

I looked over at Coriander expecting to see a look of anger or disappointment on his face, similar to his sour expression from the last time we were leaving this place. Instead, he had a sneaky smile teasing the side of his lips. His hands were deep inside his coverall pockets when he turned to me with a big grin. What was he so happy about? Maybe he was just happy to be alive, away from all the chaos. Maybe he couldn't wait to get home, and he was picturing his homecoming? What a good sport he was because I knew how much finding that treasure meant to him.

I decided to console him even though he didn't seem upset.

"Sorry we never found the treasure."

"Huh? Oh." He leaned over, speaking in an upbeat whisper, "I did find the treasure!"

"What?" I couldn't believe my own ears.

"Shhh!"

"Okay okay, what?" I whispered.

"I found it!" he quietly exclaimed.

"Are you for real?" I asked, still in disbelief.

He turned to block off any onlookers, pulled out his balled fist, and opened it. His hand was filled with large sparkling diamonds. He rolled them around then put them back in his pocket quickly.

"What? How? When? Where did you find them?" I asked.

"The mirror, after I broke it, they came spilling out. The crust, the mirror and possibly that whole cave was made out of these diamonds. I grabbed a couple of handfuls before we had to get out of there."

"How did you know to break the mirror?"

"I didn't know, actually. I just knew I couldn't let you go into the mirror with the rest of them. You would be lost forever. I tried pulling you out, but I couldn't. You were being sucked into the mirror so I grabbed the first thing I could find and smashed it. And then … well, you know the rest," Coriander concluded with a proud smile. I had never seen Coriander look so fulfilled … so accomplished … so gallant. Not only did he save my life, he found the treasure. What a great feeling! Now, what was he going to do with it???

EPILOGUE

I stared at my face in the mirror. Ginger came in and used the other sink in the big bathroom my family of seven shared.

"If you were wondering, yes, you are a sphincter," Ginger informed me as she flared her nostrils in the mirror while washing her hands. I looked at my face again and wondered when she would stop calling me that. I came up with an answer—never.

Juniper came into the bathroom, too, and we made ugly faces at each other in the mirror before we started laughing. Three sisters making ugly faces and weird noises was quite a sight. It felt good to be home even with all of Ginger's insults. I think they were her way of telling me that she liked me and maybe even loved me.

Hickory was moving out soon. He decided to sell his lawn business and go into the chocolate business. He was on his way to becoming the millionaire he had promised our father he'd be.

My dad was very proud of Hickory becoming a grown-up, and he talked about my brother's new career to everyone. The only thing my dad bragged about more than Hickory and his prize-winning sputtering, old death-trap cars, was my mom—the best part of his collection.

After I was returned home, my parents were so happy that Juniper and I were back; they threw a huge party—plus it was my birthday. They had some making up to do because my last birthday had been so unhappy.

I invited all my friends from The Children's Horrible House and Compass Academy. We had a great time playing man-hunt, eating hot dogs, deviled eggs, and chocolate cake! It was a blast seeing my friends having fun with my big goofy family.

Clover had been spending a lot of time over at my house. When her parents moved in two different directions, she decided to move in with us for the rest of the summer. Her parents reluctantly agreed but decided that until they figured everything out, our house would be the most stable environment for her.

Turns out that Staniel and Danley *were* the twins Begonia had heard of back in Buttonwood, and they weren't too far away. We kept in contact by telephone a lot.

Déjeuner went back to a fancy, special school that helped her develop more than just her sixth sense. Juniper, Clover, and I went to go visit her all the time, thanks to Hyperion, our chauffeur.

Begonia had enjoyed taking such great care of my hamsters at The Children's Horrible House, that she decided to adopt Moe when we got home. Eenie went with Déjeuner to keep her company while she was in her new school. Meenie moved with Clover after she went to live with her mother. And Miney, I gave to the twins. Coriander had enough to occupy himself with all the treasure he had found. He was kind enough to give each of our friends a giant sparkling diamond and split the rest with me. I still have all my sparkling jewels and will never part with them. They're all I have left of the time we spent at the most intriguing, spooky, charming, storied, supernatural mansion … not a bad parting gift, right?

One night after putting Cookie back in her cage, I was staring into one of the large multi-faceted diamonds when Cashew came into my room and sat on my bed.

"Did something magical happen to you? You look so pretty with your hair growing out so nicely. Looks like you're beginning to blossom!" he said with a wink.

"Thanks, Cashew." I smiled.

Even though I never found my bunny hat, I guess I didn't need it anymore. Guess being busy day and night and not having access to scissors was a good thing.

"So, how was your stay?" he asked.

"Huh?" Maybe I misunderstood him. I wasn't sure what he was talking about.

"At *The Children's Horrible House,*" he sang the tune.

"How did you know that I was there?" I sat up.

"Because when I was your age, I went there, too."

"You did?"

"Yes! That's why my room is so clean, and my bed is always made."

I looked around at my clean room, made bed, and felt a sense of pride.

"I knew Juniper went but not you, too! Did Ginger or Hickory go?" I asked.

"Their rooms and beds speak for themselves."

"Oh."

"I'm glad you're back and that your room is so clean," he said.

"Because if you don't keep it that way, you'll be heading back to:

"The Children's extra Horrible House
The Children's extra Horrible House
Where you work all day and never, never play …
The Children's extra Horrible House … ahhh!"

Wink Wink …

A NOTE FROM THE AUTHOR

It is my sincerest hope that you enjoyed reading these *HORRIBLE* books. I cannot express the glee that came over me while concocting and embellishing these stories. For those of you who do not know, The Children's Horrible House is a place where my brothers and sisters would to threaten to send me when I was Holly's age. What you read about Holly's home life is largely based on my childhood and family. I was so blessed with a large kooky family who was never afraid to be strange—mainly because we didn't know we were.

My childhood home was overstuffed with kids, (not always related) puppies, kitties, dune buggies, endless home restorations, hole digging, church, music, fun, laundry, trumpets, trombones, car shows, camping, adventures, sandwiches, lasagna, farm animals, apple orchards, vitamin parties, dishes, and unmade beds.

When it was time to clean, (when company was coming over) my poor mom was met with stubbornness and whining, mostly from me. In order to combat my obstinate ways, my siblings decided to contrive a place that sounded so horrible that no one in their right mind would choose to go. It started as The Horrible Children's House but somehow turned into The Children's Horrible House, and the name stuck along with the song they sang.

I am the youngest of five peculiar children that were brought forth from an amazingly sweet, quiet, and patient mother and a father who cannot be characterized solely on his two hobbies, cars and my mom—he was and is much more than those. His obsessions were softened by his deep devotion to the well-being of his ducklings, now grown, but never too old for a good talking to. And so, it was by my father's stern decree that I published my first book, *The Rocket Ship Bed Trip*, and for that and countless other reasons, I will always be grateful.

After a year or so, I was waiting for my next picture book to be illustrated. It was taking too long for this impatient person—me. So, I decided to take up my time by writing a book that didn't require illustrations.

What better place to bring to life than the spooky, terrible place my brothers and sisters had tricked me into believing was real? As I was writing the story, I decided that it couldn't just be horrible, it had to be fantastic and fun, too. Because having fun is my favorite!

I decided to name the director Sirius Pankins to set the tone *plus* I thought it would be funny. I had no idea that her name and the symbols I included would have been so pertinent to the outcome of the story. At times, I felt like I wasn't the only one writing these books. Someone bigger, smarter, and better had a huge hand in the story, because it worked out more synchronized than I could have planned.

If you are reading *The Children's Horrible House* books as a child or are young at heart, I hope you enjoyed this goofy, quirky, offbeat story with a side dish of science. I had such a great time reliving the many adventures I had with my family and lifetime friends.

Thank you for taking your precious time to discover, sit, read, and share these books. I hope some of these words will lead you to a forgotten or cherished nostalgic time in your life.

Fueling sweet dreams,

N. Jane Quackenbush

About the Author

N. Jane Quackenbush is a graduate of Palm Beach Atlantic University. She lives in a horrible house filled with mystery and fun in St. Augustine, Florida, a place she finds a lot of material by which she is inspired. A lot of the places mentioned in this book are based on actual haunted buildings, star-filled planetariums and magical gardens deep within The Nation's Oldest City. If you can find and name them, please let Ms. Quackenbush know by contacting her at www.hiddenwolfbooks.com.

You can also stay in touch with N. Jane Quackenbush on Facebook.

N. Jane Quackenbush has also written the following Children's Picture Books:

The Rocket Ship Bed Trip

The Pirate Ship Bed Trip

The Afternoon Moon

Middle Grade Books:

The Children's Horrible House

Return to The Children's Horrible House

Young Adult Romance:

Light in Darkness Lies

If you enjoyed reading *Escape from The Children's Horrible House*, please leave a review.

www.ingramcontent.com/pod-product-compliance
Lightning Source LLC
Chambersburg PA
CBHW020329030826
48979CB00021B/504

* 9 7 8 0 9 9 6 8 9 2 2 3 0 *